I0595007

WHEN THE PAST COMES HOME

Books By LG Rice

SECRETS OF SAGE MANOR SERIES

Through The Crystal Gate

Shadows Over Tanzlora

Battle For Pisgah

WHAT IF ETs ARE REAL?

When the Past Comes Home

LG Rice

Disclaimer

This is a work of fiction. Names, characters, places, and events are the product of the author's imagination or are used fictitiously. Any resemblance to actual persons, living or dead, or to real-life events is purely coincidental.

While this story includes references to real locations for atmospheric and narrative purposes, these references are intended solely to enhance the fictional setting and should not be interpreted as factual representations.

Copyright © 2025 by L G Rice

All rights reserved. No part of this book may be reproduced in any manner whatsoever without written permission except in the case of brief quotations embodied in critical articles and reviews.

First Printing, 2025

For those who feel caged by choices, caught between
who they are and who they want to be—
May Cassie's journey remind you that it's never too late
to rewrite your story.

Prologue

The forest always felt too close.

Even from inside the Dixon house—windows shut, curtains drawn—Cassie could feel the trees watching. They loomed just past the edge of the yard, whispering secrets in the wind. Secrets she didn't want to remember.

Seth loved it here. Galen Valley was his sanctuary. For Cassie, it had always been something else entirely.

A cage.

She used to think time could change that. That she'd wake up one day and breathe deeply without feeling trapped. That she'd forget what it felt like to be someone else. Someone with a past that still clung to her like a second skin.

But the past has a way of finding cracks. And when it does, it slips through them like smoke. Inescapable. Unforgiving.

1

Cassie Dixon opened her eyes to the soft golden glow filtering through the kitchen window. The scent of pine wafted through the screened back door, mingling with the rich bitterness of freshly brewed coffee. To anyone else, it might have seemed like the start of a perfect day.

To Cassie, it was just another morning in the prison she'd walked into willingly.

Seth was already gone—no surprise there. Her husband's job as a park ranger meant early starts and long days, most of which left her alone in their cozy but suffocating craftsman-style home on the edge of town.

Cassie sat at the kitchen table, one leg curled under her, and stared at the untouched grocery list beside her cup. She didn't want to go shopping. She didn't want to cook. She didn't even want to be *here*—in this town, in this house, in this version of her life.

She reached for her phone instead, thumbing through job alerts in Charlotte and Raleigh like she did every morning. The listings blurred into each other: marketing assistant, retail coordinator, front desk specialist. Anything sounded better than being a lonely house-wife in a town she never chose.

The ring of the wind chimes on the porch pulled her out of her thoughts. A breeze had picked up, the kind that smelled like pine and dirt and untouched wilderness. Seth loved that scent. He always said it cleared his head.

Cassie envied that. Her head never felt clear here. Only cluttered. Only trapped.

With a heavy sigh, she grabbed her canvas bag and keys.

The Galen Valley Market sat at the corner of Pine and Wisteria, nestled between the post office and a diner that still served meatloaf like it was 1962. The automatic doors whooshed open, and Cassie entered to the faint hum of fluorescent lights and the comforting scent of ground coffee beans and oranges.

She moved through the aisles on autopilot: fresh greens, vanilla oat milk, the Greek yogurt Seth liked. In the cereal section, she lingered. Not because she needed cereal—but because, somehow, it felt like the safest place to lose five minutes of her day.

That's when she noticed him.

A man, late thirties maybe, tall with sandy brown hair and a crooked smile that reached his eyes. He was trying to scan a box of granola at the self-checkout, holding it at different angles while the machine barked at him to "Please place your item in the bagging area."

Cassie smirked before she could stop herself.

He glanced up and caught her.

"Well, clearly I'm a technological wizard," he said with mock gravity.

She chuckled. "You have to lift it just enough to confuse the scale. It's practically a sport."

"Is that so?" he asked, raising an eyebrow. "You look like a seasoned pro."

"Years of grocery store battles."

"Cassie Dixon," she said automatically, before catching herself. "I mean... I'm Cassie."

"Elliot," he replied, offering a warm smile. "Elliot Rhodes. I teach drama at the high school."

Of course he did. He had that slightly disheveled, charming energy that all drama teachers seemed to possess.

Cassie nodded politely, willing her cheeks not to flush. "Well, good luck with your checkout performance."

"I'll be here all week," he quipped, waving his granola like a microphone.

She laughed, turning to push her cart away. But as she rounded the corner toward the registers, she could still feel his smile behind her.

By the time she arrived home, the sky had shifted to a soft blue, sunlight filtering in through the kitchen windows. Cassie set the grocery bags on the counter and began unpacking slowly, her thoughts far from the produce and pantry items.

Her reflection in the microwave caught her attention—eyes hollow, mouth set too tightly. She was thirty-four years old and living someone else's life.

Seth's life.

She grabbed her laptop and opened it, heart pounding as she typed in her search:

"Marketing jobs in Charlotte"

She clicked on three listings. Then four. Then opened another tab.

"Studio apartments Charlotte under $1500"

Her throat tightened. She didn't even notice the tears until they splashed onto the keyboard.

Later that night, Seth came home with mud on his boots and windburn on his cheeks, smelling like pine and leather and the trail.

"How was the day?" he asked, placing a kiss on her forehead.

Cassie forced a smile. "Quiet."

"Want to go into town tomorrow? Grab lunch at that new place next to the coffee shop?"

"Maybe. I might have some errands."

Seth didn't press. He rarely did. He was kind, dependable, gentle with her—but there was always a distance she couldn't close. She wondered if he felt it too, or if he simply chose not to.

They ate in silence. The kind of silence filled with unsaid things.

The next morning, Seth pulled on his ranger jacket while Cassie sipped her coffee.

"I'll be back late," he said. "There's a search training up in the north trailhead."

She nodded, feigning interest. "Be careful." He did not mention lunch.

He paused, studying her. "You okay?"

"I'm fine," she lied, smiling. "Just restless, I guess."

He leaned down and kissed the top of her head. "Maybe we'll take a trip. Clear your mind."

Cassie said nothing. A trip wouldn't fix what was broken.

When he left, the silence returned like a familiar guest.

She finished her coffee and glanced at the window. Beyond it lay the forest. The same one Seth adored. The one that closed in on her like walls.

She needed to get out.

Cassie found herself at the coffee shop, the Everbrew Cafe. She didn't know why she kept thinking about that smile from the grocery store.

But she did.

And when the bell above the door chimed and Elliot Rhodes walked in like a scene timed perfectly, she felt her pulse skip in recognition.

This time, he saw her first. He nodded and then got in line.

A few minutes later he walked over casually, holding two coffees. "Vanilla oat milk, right?"

Cassie blinked. "Are you psychic?"

"Just observant," he said, offering her the cup. "Thought you might need a second cup as an excuse to stay and talk."

Her fingers brushed his as she accepted it.

It was harmless.

Wasn't it?

Across town, in the sheriff's office, Seth leaned against the frame of Sheriff Marshall Bowen's door.

"I don't know what to do," he said quietly.

Marshall looked up from his paperwork. "This about Cassie?"

"She's... different lately. Distant. She talks about the city more. About leaving."

Marshall nodded slowly, leaning back. "Have you asked her what she needs?"

"I thought I *was* what she needed."

"Maybe she just hasn't found her place here yet," Marshall said. "Kathryn's been looking for help at the boutique—social media stuff. She wants to reach a younger crowd, maybe even find a model."

Marshall's wife, Kathryn, owned the Valley Vogue clothing boutique in the heart of downtown Galen Valley.

Seth looked skeptical. "Cassie doesn't really do... boutique."

"Maybe not. But Kathryn's good with people. It might give Cassie a purpose. A friend."

Seth didn't reply, but the idea clung to him like the first spark of hope he'd felt in weeks.

"Tell you what," Marshall said, "I'll talk to Kathryn and have her reach out."

That evening, Kathryn Bowen sent the message.

Kathryn (Valley Vogue): *Hey Cassie! I could use your eye—and your style. Want to help me out at the shop? We could use a boost in the Insta world. And you'd be perfect in front of the camera too. I'll pay, of course. Think about it?*

Cassie stared at the screen.

Help at a boutique? Model?

The old version of herself—before Galen Valley, before Seth, before the suffocating quiet—would've jumped at the chance. But that girl felt so far away now.

Still, her fingers hovered over the keyboard.

Maybe Kathryn was right.

Maybe it was time to find out if there was still more to her than the cage she called home.

2

The spring breeze carried a subtle scent of honeysuckle as Cassie stepped out of Valley Vogue the next afternoon. Kathryn Bowen had called that morning, asking if she had given any thought to her offer. Cassie almost declined—she didn't feel like chatting with anyone, much less posing for photos—but the way Kathryn phrased the offer made her hesitate.

"I'm desperate for a bit of guidance—and someone with your kind of look," Kathryn had said. "Stylish but natural. I'll pay you well. Think of it as... a fresh start?"

It wasn't the money that changed Cassie's mind. It was the phrase *fresh start*. It stirred something deep in her chest, something that made her consider what staying might look like if she gave Galen Valley another chance.

Cassie had met Kathryn once—at a town fundraiser, one of those polite exchanges where you smile and promise to "grab coffee sometime" and never mean it.

But Kathryn was different. Galen Valley royalty in her own right—owner of the boutique *Valley Vogue*, wife to the town's sheriff, and impeccably put-together in a way that made everyone else feel underdressed.

After an hour of sorting racks of maxi dresses and answering questions about hashtags she barely knew the answers to, she needed air.

That's how she found herself strolling along the town's cozy main strip. At this hour, the shops were just opening, and sunlight filtered through hanging planters and wooden signage, illuminating the cobblestones beneath her boots. She wasn't quite ready to go home—not yet.

Across the street, tucked between a used bookstore and the florist, sat the warm, familiar windows of Everbrew Café.

The coffee shop.

Her steps slowed, and her chest tightened. Elliot, the man from the grocery store—*his smile*—had stayed with her like an echo all night. His laugh. They had talked for less than ten minutes the day before. It was ridiculous, she told herself. Harmless. But her hand reached for the door before her brain had time to stop it.

The bell chimed as she stepped inside.

It was quiet, with only a few people scattered at tables, laptops open, earbuds in. Behind the counter, a barista with emerald-dyed hair smiled. "Morning! Just the usual?"

Cassie blinked. "Oh—I don't think I've been in enough for a usual yet."

"Well, lucky for you, I'm great at guessing," the girl said, already starting the espresso machine. "Vanilla oat milk latte?"

Cassie laughed. "Honestly? Perfect."

She wandered to a small table by the window. Her reflection in the glass caught her attention—tired eyes, minimal makeup, a scarf knotted lazily at her throat. She didn't look unhappy. Just... unsure.

And then, the door opened.

She knew it was him the moment she saw the tan messenger bag slung over his shoulder and the slight scruff on his jawline. He didn't see her at first, too busy placing an order and joking with the barista. Cassie watched him talk—effortless, warm—and tried to decide whether she should make herself visible or disappear altogether.

She didn't get the chance.

As he turned, their eyes locked, and a slow smile lit up his face.

"Hello, again."

Cassie chuckled, her cheeks flushing. "Hi."

He crossed the café and gestured to the chair opposite her. "Mind if I?"

She hesitated. "Sure. Why not?"

"So, you know what I do," he said as he settled in. "but you never told me what you do."

"Wife of a park ranger."

His brows lifted slightly. "You say that like it's a job title."

"It kind of feels like one some days," she said, then immediately regretted it. "Sorry. That sounded—"

"No need. I get it," he said, taking a sip of his coffee. "Small towns can feel... small. Especially if you're not from here."

Cassie glanced out the window, her voice quiet. "I keep trying to make it feel like home. It just never sticks."

Elliot didn't press. He just nodded like someone who'd heard versions of the same thing before. "It takes time. Or the right kind of distraction."

The comment hung in the air between them, not inappropriate, not innocent either. Cassie laughed softly, choosing to ignore the implications.

Elliot was magnetic, the kind of person who made you feel interesting just by looking at you like you mattered.

They talked for nearly half an hour. Books. Music. Big city life. Small town weirdness.

It was harmless.

She told herself it was harmless.

And when she finally stood to leave, she felt a flicker of something unsettling: disappointment.

Across town, Seth leaned against the patrol truck outside the sheriff's office, arms crossed as he watched Marshall approach.

"She's pulling away," Seth said before Marshall could speak. "And I don't know how to stop it."

Marshall, ever calm, adjusted the brim of his hat and leaned on the hood beside him. "Cassie?"

Seth nodded.

"She hates it here," he added, eyes locked on the sidewalk. "Hated it from the minute we unpacked. I thought she'd adjust. I thought I'd be enough."

Marshall didn't say anything right away. He knew better than to jump in too fast. After a beat, he said, "Sometimes people don't hate the place. Sometimes they just haven't found their place in it yet."

Seth looked over. "You think that's all it is?"

"I think there's more going on than she's saying," Marshall replied carefully. "Kathryn's asked her for help with Valley Vogue's online stuff. Maybe Cassie will agree."

Seth straightened, surprised. "She did not mention anything about that to me."

"Well, you don't mention it to her," Marshall said with a knowing grin. "Let Kathryn work her magic. She's persuasive."

3

———————————————

Cassie adjusted the floral blouse Kathryn had given her to try on, tugging the hem nervously as she turned to face the mirror in the boutique's fitting area. The soft lighting inside Valley Vogue made everything feel more flattering—gentler, more forgiving. Kathryn had told her she had "that classic face—elegant but real," and for a moment, Cassie believed her.

Still, the unfamiliar reflection staring back made her skin itch. It wasn't just the clothes. It was this town, this new role, the attention. She wasn't used to being seen.

"You look amazing," Kathryn said from behind her phone as she snapped a photo. "Seriously. You're a natural. Look at this!"

Cassie stepped forward as Kathryn flipped the phone around. There she was—shoulders back, chin up, a wry smile tugging at her lips.

"That doesn't even look like me," Cassie murmured.

"That *is* you," Kathryn said firmly. "That's the version of you Galen Valley needs to meet."

Cassie didn't answer. She didn't know how to explain that every time someone complimented her here, it felt like they were talking to a character she was still auditioning for.

Kathryn, sensing her hesitation, softened her voice. "I know this town can feel a little… tight. But you've got something special, Cassie. People will see that if you let them."

Cassie nodded absently, her gaze drifting toward the front window. She could see the street from here—the benches where old men smoked cigars and argued about fishing, the flower cart that always tilted slightly to the left, and just beyond that... the entrance to Ever-brew Café.

Her pulse quickened.

She hadn't seen Elliot since their last coffee shop run-in, but she hadn't stopped thinking about him either. His voice, his laugh, the way he leaned in like he actually cared what she had to say. That kind of attention was intoxicating. Dangerous.

Kathryn's voice broke through her thoughts. "Do you want to take a quick break before we shoot the next look?"

Cassie blinked. "Yeah. That'd be great."

She stepped out the back door into the alley that separated the boutique from the bookstore. The sun had warmed the bricks, and the scent of lavender from the planter beside her was oddly comforting.

She needed air. Clarity.

Instead, she pulled out her phone and opened her messages.

No new texts from Seth.

But there *was* one from an unknown number.

Unknown: *Cassie. Didn't expect to see your name in a place like this. Call me. We need to talk.*

Her blood ran cold.

She stared at the message, fingers frozen. There was no name, but she knew who it was.

There was only one person who could cut through her like that with so few words.

Meanwhile, at Galen Valley High, Elliot Rhodes leaned over his desk, shuffling through rehearsal notes while the hum of fluorescent lights buzzed overhead. His students had cleared out hours ago, but he wasn't ready to go home. Not yet.

He reached for his phone, almost against his better judgment.

No texts from Cassie even though they had exchanged numbers.

He hadn't expected one, but still... he felt the sting of silence.

"Still here?"

He looked up to see Margaret Holloway, the English teacher from across the hall, lingering in his doorway with a knowing smile.

"Yeah. Figured I'd get a head start on next week's rehearsal notes."

Margaret raised an eyebrow as she stepped inside. "Rehearsal notes or brooding over that pretty blonde from the coffee shop?"

Elliot sighed. "You don't miss much, do you?"

"Forty-two years in education, Elliot. Kids aren't the only ones I read like open books."

He tried to deflect with humor. "So what's my tragic backstory then?"

"More like tragic present," she said gently, pulling up a chair. "She's married, isn't she?"

Elliot looked away.

Margaret folded her hands. "You don't have to say anything. But I saw the way she looked at you. And the way *you* looked at *her*. I've seen that look before. It never ends without someone getting hurt."

"She's unhappy," Elliot said quietly. "She doesn't say it, not outright. But it's there. She's—trapped."

"Maybe," Margaret replied. "Or maybe she just hasn't told you the whole story."

Elliot frowned. "You think I'm being stupid."

"I think you're romanticizing someone you barely know. And I think you're a good man who's about to do something that could change everything—not just for you, but for her."

Elliot didn't respond. He couldn't. Because part of him knew she was right.

But the other part didn't care.

Cassie sat in her car behind Valley Vogue, phone still in her hand, heart thundering against her ribcage.

That number had no business finding her.

She hadn't spoken to Devon Blake in over three years—not since she'd left Chicago and buried that version of herself in a box she swore never to open.

She should block him. Delete the message. Pretend it never came.

Instead, her fingers trembled as she called the number.

He picked up on the first ring.

"Well, well. The ghost returns," Devon said smoothly. "Didn't think I'd actually hear your voice again."

"I can't talk long," she said. "How did you find me?"

"You always did underestimate me," he said. "A mutual acquaintance tipped me off. Imagine my surprise when I found out little Cassie Stringfield had turned into some kind of model in a town that doesn't even have Uber."

"What do you want?"

"I want to see you," Devon said. "You owe me that much."

"I don't owe you *anything*."

"Don't kid yourself. You know what we left unfinished."

Cassie's throat tightened. "I moved on."

Devon's voice softened, but not kindly. "I wonder if your husband knows the real reason you left Chicago. Wonder if your new town would be so welcoming if they knew what you did."

Cassie's silence said everything.

Devon waited a beat, then added, "Tomorrow. Noon. Behind the fire station. Don't make me come looking."

He hung up.

Cassie stared at her reflection in the rearview mirror. For a moment, she didn't recognize the woman staring back.

The boutique model. The doting wife. The almost-cheater.

No. None of those were her.

She was someone with a past.

And it was knocking.

That night, Seth returned home earlier than expected. Cassie was curled on the couch, wine glass in hand, eyes glazed over as the flicker of a muted TV danced across her face.

"Hey," he said softly, sitting beside her. "You okay?"

She blinked. "Yeah. Just tired."

He ran a hand down her arm. "Marshall told me Kathryn asked you to help at the boutique. That's... great, Cass. You said you wanted to do something, and this is perfect."

She offered a faint smile. "It was fine."

"That's all?"

"Yeah." She stood abruptly. "I'm going to take a bath."

Seth watched her walk down the hallway, the distance between them growing by the second. He wanted to follow. To ask more. To hold her.

But something told him not to.

Something told him she wasn't just tired.

She was slipping away.

The next morning, Elliot parked outside the boutique just as Cassie stepped out, head down, arms wrapped tightly around herself despite the mild weather.

She didn't see him until he spoke. "You okay?"

Cassie looked up sharply. "What are you doing here?"

"Honestly? Hoping to run into you."

"I have somewhere to be."

He hesitated. "Did I do something?"

Cassie's eyes flicked toward him, and for a moment, he saw something raw behind them—fear, maybe. Or guilt. Or both.

"You didn't do anything," she said. "But this—whatever it is—we can't."

Elliot stepped closer. "Cassie—"

"No," she said, firmer now. "You're a good guy, Elliot. Don't make this harder."

And with that, she walked away, leaving him standing in the morning sunlight, watching her disappear.

4

Cassie stood behind the old fire station, her back pressed against the red brick wall, the morning sun doing little to chase away the cold sweat clinging to her skin.

He appeared ten minutes late—because of course he did—wearing the same arrogant smirk that used to thrill her and now only made her stomach churn.

"Well," he said, sunglasses sliding down his nose as he looked her over. "Time's been kind to you."

"Say what you came to say."

Devon chuckled. "Straight to business. No hug for old times' sake?"

Cassie didn't flinch. "You lost the right to 'old times' when you threatened me."

"I didn't threaten you," he said, leaning against the wall beside her. "I reminded you. There's a difference."

"Why now?"

"Because," Devon said, taking a slow drag of a cigarette he pulled from behind his ear, "a friend of mine saw your little 'boutique model' debut on social media. Guess small-town Cassie didn't stay buried like you promised."

"You don't get to guilt me for starting over."

"I wouldn't bother," he said coolly. "You've always been good at running. But you forget—some of us remember the version of you that got messy. Dangerous."

Cassie's jaw clenched. "That girl is gone."

"She's not," he said, exhaling smoke between his teeth. "She's just dressed up in pastels and pretending to be someone's perfect wife."

Cassie's breath caught. "I didn't do anything illegal."

Devon turned to face her fully now, his smile dark. "Didn't you?"

Her silence was answer enough.

He took a step forward. "I'm not here to ruin your little Hallmark life. But I'm also not leaving town just yet. Not until we've had a real talk. I think you owe me at least that."

"I don't owe you anything," Cassie whispered, her voice trembling. "You were just as guilty."

"Maybe," he said. "But only one of us started a new life with a different name."

Cassie froze. "You wouldn't."

Devon smirked. "Wouldn't I?"

He pulled something from his coat pocket—a flash drive. "I have copies. Emails. Photos. A full paper trail."

Cassie's stomach dropped.

"You release that and you burn too."

"I'm not the one with a husband and a PR problem."

"You wouldn't."

Devon smirked. "Let's not find out."

Across town, Elliot sat across from Margaret Holloway at her usual booth in Everbrew Café. His face was pale, jaw tight.

"She told me to walk away," he said quietly.

Margaret stirred her tea. "Then maybe you should."

"I can't. Not like this. She's scared."

"Scared people are unpredictable," Margaret replied. "So are men in love."

"I'm not—" Elliot stopped, realizing the lie before it even finished forming. "It's not love. It's... I see her."

"You see who she wants you to see," Margaret corrected gently. "But who is she when she's not performing?"

Elliot rubbed a hand over his face. "I thought she was just stuck. But now I think she's hiding."

Margaret gave a sad smile. "Sometimes those are the same thing."

At Valley Vogue, Kathryn Bowen moved hangers around without much thought, more preoccupied by her phone than the spring inventory. Cassie was late. She'd said she'd be in by ten. It was half past.

It wasn't like Cassie to bail—especially not after such a strong start.

Kathryn considered texting her, but something told her to wait.

Instead, she walked to the boutique's front window and stared across the street at Everbrew Café, where she caught sight of Elliot Rhodes deep in conversation with Margaret Holloway.

A flicker of suspicion stirred.

Kathryn had a nose for drama. It came with the territory of owning a boutique in a town where everyone knew everything. And lately, Cassie's life felt like it was humming with something beneath the surface.

Cassie finally arrived just before noon, breathless and visibly shaken.

Kathryn noticed immediately.

"You look like you've seen a ghost," she said gently.

Cassie offered a weak smile. "Something like that."

"Want to talk about it?"

"No," Cassie said too quickly, then added, "Not yet."

Kathryn nodded and handed her a silk wrap dress. "Why don't you slip into this and we'll just ease into the shoot. No pressure."

Cassie disappeared into the back, grateful for the escape. But as she stood before the boutique's mirror, draped in designer silk and bathed in soft light, her mind wasn't on fashion or poses.

It was on Devon.

On the secret he carried like a loaded gun.

And the very real possibility that it could detonate her entire life.

That evening, Seth stood outside the sheriff's office again, this time gripping the edge of the truck bed with white knuckles. Marshall leaned beside him, watching him carefully.

"She's somewhere else lately," Seth said. "I don't mean physically—I mean her mind. Her heart. It's not here."

"You talk to her?"

"She says she's fine. But it's like I'm talking to a wall."

Marshall nodded. "I hate to say it, but you might have to stop trying to fix it and just listen."

"I *have* been listening."

"Then maybe you need to hear what she's not saying."

Seth exhaled, defeated. "I feel like I'm losing her."

Marshall clapped a hand on his shoulder. "Then fight for her. Just don't smother her. People run when they can't breathe."

That night, Cassie poured a second glass of wine before making her way to the bedroom. Seth was reading in bed, glasses perched on the bridge of his nose, a bookmark between his fingers.

"You working tomorrow?" she asked, sitting beside him.

"Nope," he said. "Taking the day off."

She blinked. "Really?"

"Yeah. Thought maybe we could do something. Go for a drive. Have lunch. Just us."

Cassie hesitated. "That sounds… nice."

He looked at her then, really looked. "Cass, is everything okay?"

She met his eyes—and in them, saw all the things she used to love about him: his loyalty, his gentleness, his complete inability to lie.

But she couldn't bring herself to be honest.

"Yeah," she whispered. "Just tired."

He nodded and set his book aside. "Come here."

She slid under the covers beside him, letting his arms wrap around her. For a few moments, she let herself believe this could be enough.

But in the dark, her mind drifted to Elliot.

And Devon.

And the life she'd spent so long trying to forget.

The next morning, she slipped out of bed early and walked to the edge of the woods behind their house. The pine trees loomed tall and indifferent, casting long shadows across the moss-covered ground.

She needed to make a decision.

Devon wouldn't wait forever—and neither would her secrets.

Just as she turned to go, a voice startled her.

"You come out here a lot?"

Cassie whipped around to find Elliot standing several feet away, hands in his pockets, eyes shadowed with uncertainty.

"I needed air," she said.

He nodded. "Me too."

They stood in silence, the forest buzzing softly with birdsong and breeze.

"I shouldn't be here," he said finally. "You told me to walk away."

Cassie looked at him. "I know."

"Then why do you keep looking at me like you don't want me to?"

She opened her mouth—then closed it again.

"I'm married," she said. "I'm not proud of what I've been feeling."

"I'm not asking you to be proud," he said. "I'm asking you to be honest."

Cassie blinked back the sudden sting in her eyes. "I've made mistakes, Elliot. Big ones. And if I tell you who I really am—if I let you see it—you won't want any part of it."

"You don't know that."

"Yes, I do."

Elliot took a step closer. "Try me."

5

Elliot stood frozen, heart thudding beneath the pine-filtered light of the woods, staring at Cassie as if seeing her for the first time.

She hadn't moved since her confession.

"I wasn't just running from the city," she'd said. "I was running from something I did. Something that could ruin everything."

Now, she waited—jaw tight, hands clenched—like someone bracing for the punch they knew was coming.

Elliot's voice was hoarse. "What did you do?"

Cassie looked down, unable to meet his eyes. "There was a man. Someone I was with... before Seth. His name was Devon."

"Is this the same guy—?"

"The one who messaged me, yes."

"What does he want?"

Cassie hesitated. "He wants to remind me who I used to be. Or... punish me for leaving that version of myself behind."

Elliot took a step forward. "Cassie, if he's threatening you—"

"I'm not in danger," she interrupted. "At least... not the way you think. Devon doesn't want to hurt me physically. He wants to control the narrative. Make sure I never forget what happened."

Elliot's brows knit. "What *did* happen?"

Cassie closed her eyes. "We were part of something. An event—some people would call it a scheme. It was meant to expose a shady investor tied to a nonprofit I worked for. But it went too far. Someone got hurt. Not because of me—not directly. But my hands weren't clean. And Devon... he had the connections to bury it. For both of us."

"Cassie…" Elliot's voice softened. "Why didn't you ever tell Seth?"

She laughed bitterly. "Because Seth sees the world in black and white. Right and wrong. He married the woman I pretended to be, not the one who helped orchestrate a media scandal and fled under a different last name."

Elliot was quiet for a long moment, and when he finally spoke, his words cut deep.

"So what does that make *me*? Your escape? Your next alias?"

Cassie flinched. "No. You were… unexpected. And honest. And I didn't think I'd feel anything again—until I met you."

He looked at her, torn between compassion and caution. "I can't be your secret, Cassie. I won't."

"I know," she whispered. "That's why I'm telling you the truth now."

Elliot didn't respond. He just nodded, then turned and walked back toward the trail, leaving her alone in the stillness, surrounded by trees—and everything she hadn't wanted to remember.

At Valley Vogue, Kathryn Bowen unlocked the back storage room door, humming along to the faint strains of Fleetwood Mac playing overhead. She was pulling spring inventory for next week's window display when something caught her eye: a tote bag that didn't belong to her.

Cassie's.

She reached inside, planning to set it aside, when her hand brushed against a worn manila envelope. Frowning, Kathryn pulled it out and opened it instinctively—then immediately regretted it.

Inside were old newspaper clippings from Chicago. Headlines with words like *"Nonprofit Scandal," "Whistleblower Vanishes,"* and *"Investigators Suspect Inside Job."*

Cassie's name wasn't mentioned—but her face was unmistakable in one photo. Standing beside a man Kathryn didn't recognize. Laughing.

Her stomach twisted.

She didn't mean to pry. But now that she had... how could she *not* ask questions?

That evening, Seth sat on their back porch, tossing peanuts to the blue jays and sipping beer. He'd cleaned the grill even though they weren't having guests, just for something to do.

Cassie hadn't spoken much since yesterday, and the space between them felt like miles.

When she finally joined him, her eyes looked tired. Not from lack of sleep—but from carrying something heavy.

"I think we need to talk," she said, sitting beside him.

He nodded, bracing himself. "Okay."

"I've been keeping something from you," she began slowly. "Something big."

Seth stiffened, but said nothing.

"I wasn't completely honest about why I left Chicago," she continued. "There was a situation... at my job. Things got messy, and I made choices I'm not proud of. I left before it could follow me. And I never told you because I thought I could bury it."

He stared straight ahead. "What kind of situation?"

Cassie took a shaky breath. "There was an exposé we helped plant. Information leaked that hurt people—some deserved it, some didn't. Devon was the one who orchestrated most of it. But I was involved. And when things started to go sideways... I panicked."

Seth's jaw clenched. "Were you charged?"

"No. But I was questioned. I left before they could build a case."

Silence.

"I didn't tell you because I didn't want you to see me differently," she said softly. "Because I wanted to believe I could be the person you think I am."

Seth exhaled slowly. "Cass, I married you because I love you. Not because I thought you were perfect."

"But I've been lying."

"You've been *pretending*," he corrected. "And that hurts worse."

Tears welled in her eyes. "I'm sorry."

Seth stood. "I don't know what to do with this. I need time."

She nodded, knowing she deserved that—and maybe more.

At Everbrew Café the next morning, Kathryn waited for Margaret Holloway with two cappuccinos and a tabloid-thin envelope in her purse.

"Didn't expect to see you looking this tense," Margaret said, sliding into the booth.

"I need advice," Kathryn said, glancing around before lowering her voice. "And maybe some perspective."

Margaret arched a brow. "This wouldn't happen to involve a certain boutique assistant, would it?"

Kathryn blinked. "You know?"

"I know *everything*, Kathryn. It's a teacher's curse."

Kathryn handed over the envelope. "I found these in Cassie's bag. I wasn't snooping, not really. But now I don't know what to do."

Margaret flipped through the clippings, her expression unreadable.

Finally, she said, "Cassie Dixon's not who this town thinks she is."

"I know. But I *like* her. And I think she wants to change."

"Then let her."

"What if people find out?"

"People always find out," Margaret said. "But if you stand by her—if we do—it gives her a fighting chance."

Kathryn nodded slowly. "So we protect her?"

"No," Margaret said, sipping her cappuccino. "We *watch* her. And when the next piece falls, we decide if she's worth saving."

Elliot stood outside the school theater, script pages in hand, when Cassie's voice called out behind him.

"I wasn't sure you'd still speak to me."

He turned. "I'm not sure I should."

She stepped closer. "I told Seth. About everything. About Devon. The nonprofit. The whole thing."

Elliot searched her face. "How'd he take it?"

"He didn't throw me out," she said. "But I'm not sure he's staying either."

He exhaled. "I meant what I said—I can't be your secret."

"You're not. Not anymore."

Silence.

"I'm not asking for anything," she said. "Not today. I just... I wanted you to know."

Elliot nodded, jaw tense. "I care about you, Cassie. But caring isn't enough if I don't know who I'm caring *about*."

Cassie swallowed hard. "Then let me prove it. Let me be better."

And with that, she walked away—again.

Seth didn't expect to find them together.

He'd been walking back from the Sheriff's station when he spotted Cassie in the alley behind the firehouse. Not alone.

The man—Devon—was too close. Cassie was stiff, pale, panicked. Seth's instincts took over.

"Hey!" he shouted, rushing toward them. "What the hell is going on?"

Devon turned with a predator's smile. "You must be the husband."

"And you are?"

"An old friend. Just catching up."

Seth didn't wait for more. He swung.

His fist connected with Devon's jaw, the crack echoing off the bricks. Cassie screamed.

Devon didn't fall. He just staggered, wiped his mouth, and chuckled darkly. "Now that's more like it."

"Go to the car," Seth told Cassie.

She didn't move.

"*Now,* Cass."

And she did.

That night, she sat on the edge of their bed, unable to meet Seth's eyes.

"I should've told you sooner," she said quietly. "About Chicago. About him."

"Yeah," Seth said, his voice tight. "You should've."

Cassie took a shaky breath. "There was an investigation. At my old job. We leaked documents to expose the corruption, but it got messy. People got hurt. Devon helped cover it up—and he never let me forget it."

"Were you charged?"

"No. But I left before they could try."

Seth stared at her. "How much of our marriage has been built on lies?"

"It wasn't a lie," she whispered. "I just... I didn't know how to tell you without losing you."

Seth stood. "You lost me the moment you kept him a secret."

Cassie blinked, stunned.

"I need space," he said. "Pack a bag."

6

It was early—too early for visitors.

Kathryn Bowen nearly dropped her coffee as the boutique's motion sensor chimed. She crossed the polished hardwood floor of *Valley Vogue* with her phone still in hand, assuming it was her delivery guy coming too early again.

But there was no one at the door.

Only a plain manila envelope.

No name. No note.

Just sealed and slightly creased like it had been passed through too many hands.

Frowning, she crouched down, picked it up, and carried it back behind the counter. She opened it cautiously, half-expecting receipts or another anonymous donation to her boutique's community closet.

What she pulled out instead made her stomach twist.

A photo—grainy, clearly taken from a distance, but unmistakable.

Cassie. With Elliot.

Not touching, not even seated too close. But the expressions on their faces? The laughter in their posture, the lean of their bodies toward each other? It was intimacy. Captured like evidence.

The second image was worse.

Cassie. At the fire station alleyway.

And a man Kathryn didn't recognize—but whose body language was threatening, possessive.

Two photos. No note. No context.

Just enough to crack the calm of Galen Valley.

Across town, Elliot stared blankly at his laptop in the darkened theater, rehearsal notes forgotten. He hadn't been able to sleep. His thoughts were tangled in Cassie's voice, her secrets, the way she looked at him when she thought he might walk away.

He was just about to close his laptop when a knock echoed from the stage door.

He opened it to find Kathryn standing there, eyes tight, envelope in hand.

"We need to talk," she said.

They sat in the back row of the theater, the dusty air heavy between them.

Kathryn handed him the envelope without a word.

Elliot pulled out the photos, jaw tightening as he flipped through them.

He didn't ask where they came from. He already knew.

"Is this what I think it is?" Kathryn asked, voice careful.

"I don't know what you think it is," Elliot replied. "But I can tell you it's complicated."

Kathryn gave him a look. "You're involved with a married woman who might have a blackmail target on her back. That's not complicated, Elliot. That's dangerous."

"She told me everything."

Kathryn raised a skeptical brow. "Everything?"

Elliot hesitated. "Enough."

Kathryn sighed, folding her hands. "Look, I like Cassie. But this town doesn't forgive easily. You need to be careful, not just for your sake—but for hers."

Elliot stared at the stage, memories rushing forward.

"I think she came here to be someone else," he said quietly. "And now the past won't let her."

Kathryn stood. "No one gets to start over without a cost."

Kathryn was sweeping the shop floor when Cassie arrived, hair still damp from a hurried shower, face blotchy with tears.

"I'm sorry to barge in," she said. "But I didn't know where else to go."

Kathryn put down the broom and crossed the room without hesitation. "Come in."

Cassie nodded, throat too tight to speak.

Kathryn led her to the back room. "We'll figure this out."

Cassie collapsed into the chair and buried her face in her hands.

She told Kathryn everything.

"I didn't know where else to go," Cassie said.

"You're here," Kathryn replied, stepping aside. "That's enough."

By the next morning, everyone in Galen Valley knew something was wrong.

At Valley Vogue, the usual quiet buzz of customers and gossip was replaced with a thick, uneasy silence. Two regulars who always chatted about fashion trends and their daughters' softball team left without buying a thing. The third whispered something to the barista at Everbrew Cafe, who in turn relayed it to her boyfriend, who texted his cousin, who sent it to his group chat.

By lunchtime, the rumors had evolved.

Cassie Dixon was a cheater.

Cassie Dixon had a criminal past.

Cassie Dixon was about to be run out of town.

And Cassie? She was hiding in the backroom of the boutique with her knees pulled to her chest, staring at her phone, debating whether to delete every piece of her online existence.

Kathryn peeked in, holding a mug of tea. "You okay?"

"No," Cassie said, voice hollow. "They know."

"Some of them think they know," Kathryn said. "There's a difference."

Cassie took the mug with shaking hands. "How do you do it?"

"Do what?"

"Live here. With everyone watching. Everyone knowing your business."

Kathryn smiled softly. "Because I made peace with the fact that people will talk no matter what. So I gave them something good to talk about."

Cassie gave a bitter laugh. "That ship has sailed."

"No," Kathryn said. "It hasn't. Not yet."

She pulled out her phone and dialed. "We're not going to fight fire with silence. We're going to fight it with strategy."

Cassie looked up. "Who are you calling?"

"Someone who understands the power of narrative."

Margaret Holloway answered the phone on the second ring, already halfway through her morning crossword.

"Let me guess," she said before Kathryn could speak. "This is about Cassie."

"I need your help," Kathryn said. "She's unraveling. And the town's turning on her."

Margaret sighed. "I warned Elliot. I told him the fallout was coming."

"Well, it's here," Kathryn said. "And we don't have time to wait for it to pass."

There was a pause, followed by the scrape of a chair. "Come to the school. After rehearsal. I have an idea."

Meanwhile, Seth stood in front of the ranger station, running his hand over the back of his neck as Marshall Bowen leaned against the porch railing.

"She's not at home," Seth said quietly.

"You told her to leave."

"I didn't tell her where to go."

Marshall tilted his head. "You worried?"

"I don't know what I am," Seth admitted. "Part of me's still angry. But part of me... still wants her to come back."

"Anger's easy," Marshall said. "What you do with it? That's the hard part."

Seth didn't respond.

Marshall took a slow sip from his thermos. "If you want her back, you're gonna have to decide if you're willing to accept the truth she finally told you—and everything that comes with it."

"And if I can't?"

"Then you let her go."

At the high school auditorium, Elliot paced the back of the stage while his students ran lines. He was distracted—again—and it wasn't going unnoticed.

Margaret entered just before the final scene wrapped up, waiting patiently until the kids filed out. Elliot didn't even turn around when he spoke.

"Another intervention?"

"No," Margaret said. "A proposition."

He finally turned. "What kind?"

She held up a folder. "An interview. With Cassie. Published in *The Galen Gazette*. Full transparency. Her story. Her words."

Elliot blinked. "You want her to go public?"

"I want her to get ahead of the narrative before Devon decides to burn it all down."

"You think she'll agree?"

Margaret shrugged. "I think she's desperate enough to try."

Cassie stared at the paper in her lap, heart racing.

Her story. Her version. In the local paper.

It felt like a trap.

But when Margaret placed a hand over hers and said, "You get to choose the headline," something inside her cracked.

"I've run from it for so long," Cassie whispered. "What if I don't like who I see when I finally stop?"

Margaret leaned back. "Then you rewrite the ending."

That night, Devon leaned against the hood of his rental car just outside the gas station on Route 17. A smirk played on his lips as he scrolled through the copy of the article Kathryn had leaked to the Gazette's editor before Cassie's interview could even be finalized.

So the little ghost *did* want to fight back.

Cute.

He clicked open a folder on his phone—images, emails, screenshots of her involvement in the scandal. Evidence he'd kept as insurance. And if she thought a cute confession in a small-town paper would erase all that?

She was in for a rude awakening.

The next morning, the Gazette published a teaser on their homepage:

COMING THIS WEEK: *"Cassie Dixon: Her Story, Her Past, and Why She's Not Running Anymore"*

Cassie read it with trembling fingers.

The town's reaction was immediate.

Half a dozen texts. Four voicemails. A few supportive messages… and several that made her sick to her stomach.

But she held firm.

Until Devon sent the final blow.

A forwarded email thread between Cassie and a whistleblower from the nonprofit—an email that could reopen a long-dormant investigation.

And at the bottom, his message:

You want to play public? Let's go all in.

Elliot found Cassie pacing in the alley behind the boutique, tears streaming down her face.

"He's going to leak it," she said. "The emails. The evidence. Everything."

Elliot took her face in his hands. "Then let him."

She blinked. "What?"

"You're not that person anymore, Cassie. You made a mistake. You tried to fix it. You've built a new life—and now you're trying to do the right thing."

"No one will believe me."

"I do," he said.

She leaned into his chest, and for a moment, all the noise disappeared.

Inside the boutique, Kathryn closed her laptop after printing the final draft of Cassie's interview. She handed it to Margaret, who gave it one last glance.

"You think it'll be enough?" Kathryn asked.

"No," Margaret said. "But it's a start."

7

Cassie hadn't slept.

She sat curled in a chair by the front window of Kathryn's boutique, cradling a lukewarm cup of coffee as the sunrise painted soft streaks of gold over Galen Valley. The streets were still empty, quiet in that delicate in-between time—before dog walkers and old men with newspapers emerged, before shops opened and gossip took to the sidewalks.

The article was live.

Margaret had sent her a text just after midnight with the link.

"Cassie Dixon: The Woman Behind the Scandal"

An exclusive look at the woman Galen Valley thought it knew—and the past she thought she'd outrun.

The headline was gentle, even redemptive. The story itself was raw and honest—edited carefully by Margaret to protect Cassie's legal standing but still true in its essence.

She'd owned her past.

Every word on that page had been Cassie's.

But now... the town would decide what to do with it.

By nine a.m., Everbrew Café was packed.

People weren't just ordering coffee anymore—they were lingering. Reading on their phones. Whispers curled around every table.

"She admitted it?"

"Do you think it's all true?"

37

"I heard she was using a fake name…"

"Wonder what Seth thinks."

By noon, the entire town had an opinion.

By three, the opinions started turning ugly.

Kathryn came back from her lunch break pale and tense.

"Someone spray-painted 'Fraud' on the alley wall behind the shop."

Cassie flinched. "I'll clean it."

"No, you won't," Kathryn said firmly. "I already called the city. They'll handle it. You don't need to take on every consequence of the past like it's penance."

Cassie wanted to believe her. But the look in people's eyes to-day—the quick glances, the sudden silences—felt a lot like punishment.

Seth saw the article, too.

He read it twice, then printed it and folded it into quarters like something sacred.

He didn't know how he felt.

He didn't feel betrayed—not anymore. She hadn't lied to hurt him. She'd lied to survive. To rebuild.

And that knowledge haunted him.

He wanted to storm over to the boutique and tell her she wasn't alone. That he still loved her. That he could still see a life together.

But he didn't move.

He just stared at the folded paper in his lap and wondered if too much damage had already been done.

Devon watched the town implode from the safety of a diner two towns over.

He scrolled through comment sections and Facebook posts with a satisfied smirk. People were already spinning Cassie's confession into something darker.

But he wasn't done.

That evening, he slid a USB drive across a café table to a journalist from a national news blog.

"You want a follow-up?" he asked. "I've got a bombshell for you."

At Valley Vogue, the phone rang off the hook—reporters, customers canceling appointments, old clients of Kathryn's pretending to be "concerned."

Kathryn stopped answering.

Instead, she handed Cassie her favorite wrap dress, her favorite lipstick, and pulled out the boutique camera.

"We're taking back the narrative," she said. "Smile like you belong here. Because you *do.*"

Cassie stepped in front of the backdrop.

And she smiled.

But the peace didn't last.

Just after sunset, Elliot's phone buzzed.

A forwarded news alert. The journalist Devon had met with had published the leaked emails.

Former Nonprofit Employee Implicated in Political Smear Campaign: Cassie Dixon at the Center of Scandal

There were photos.

There were names.

There was no turning back now.

Seth stood at the kitchen sink, staring blankly at the pile of dishes he'd been meaning to wash for two days. He hadn't turned on the TV, hadn't opened his laptop. The silence in the house was almost sacred after everything that had unraveled.

Then came the knock at the door.

He blinked, dried his hands, and crossed the living room.

Standing on the porch was Baxter Ross, lead investigator at the sheriff's department—and one of the only people Seth had trusted since high school.

In his hand: a twelve-pack of beer.

"Figured you could use a couple of cold ones," Baxter said.

Seth stepped aside. "You figured right."

They settled into the back porch chairs, the ones Cassie had hated because they squeaked whenever you leaned back too far.

Baxter cracked a can open and passed it over.

"Word's getting around," he said after a long sip. "About the mess. About Cassie. About *you.*"

Seth raised a brow. "What kind of word?"

"The usual mix of nonsense and half-truths," Baxter said. "But I'll tell you this—those of us who *know* you? We're not buying it."

Seth leaned back, beer in hand. "I appreciate that."

Baxter looked at him seriously. "More than that, Seth. If you ever need someone to back you up, you've got friends. Don't forget it."

There was a pause before Baxter added, "Sheriff's been cracking down on the gossip hard. Threatening anyone and everyone who even breathes a rumor inside the station."

Seth gave a dry chuckle. "That's comforting."

"Or suspicious," Baxter muttered. "Either way… just know I've got your six. Always have."

They sat in silence for a few minutes, sipping beer and listening to the distant creak of the pines.

For the first time in days, Seth didn't feel entirely alone.

8

Cassie didn't need to read the article to know what it said.

She only needed to see the panic in Kathryn's eyes as she burst into the backroom of *Valley Vogue*, phone in hand.

"It's out," Kathryn said, breathless. "The emails. All of them."

Cassie's knees went weak.

She reached for the edge of the table to steady herself as the blood drained from her face. "Devon."

Kathryn nodded grimly. "He sold the story. National blog. And it's already being picked up."

Cassie didn't ask for the link. She didn't need the details. The headlines were enough. Her phone buzzed relentlessly—messages from numbers she didn't recognize, notifications from people she hadn't spoken to in years.

Some offered support.

Most didn't.

By midday, the phones at the sheriff's station were ringing nonstop.

Marshall stepped out of his office to find two deputies arguing with a reporter from a news outlet in Charlotte who had driven down "just to get a feel for the town."

"We're not giving a statement," Marshall said coolly. "And if you harass any of our residents, we *will* press charges."

The reporter left reluctantly.

Marshall turned to his staff. "Can someone please get Ranger Dixon on the phone for me?"

Five minutes passed.

"His deputy rangers haven't seen him since early this morning," one of his investigators said as they stood inside the sheriff's office door. "They think he might've taken off on the north trail. It appears his radio is off or out of the service area."

Marshall sighed.

He knew where to find him.

Seth stood at the edge of the overlook off Wren Ridge, hands in his jacket pockets, eyes fixed on the valley below.

He hadn't turned his phone on since last night.

Didn't need to.

He knew.

The air was cooler up here. Still. Quiet.

And he needed that silence to think.

Because no matter how angry he'd been—how blindsided, how heartbroken—the idea of Cassie facing this alone made something primal in him ache.

She'd made mistakes.

But so had he.

She'd lied. He'd retreated. She'd fallen for someone else. He'd shut her out.

Maybe they were both to blame. Maybe neither of them was.

But one thing was clear: if he didn't act soon, he might lose her for good.

A truck engine rumbled behind him.

Seth didn't turn as it pulled up.

A door opened. Then boots on gravel.

"Didn't expect to find you all the way up here," said Marshall, stepping up beside him, arms crossed, stance solid as always.

Seth gave a humorless shrug. "Didn't expect to be the town's favorite punchline this week either."

Marshall exhaled through his nose. "That'll pass. People love a scandal, but they get bored just as fast."

"They're not bored yet."

"No," Marshall admitted. "But you can make it easier for her."

Seth turned to him, brow furrowed.

"She's getting torn up in the press—by locals, the internet, that ghost of a scandal in Chicago. But it's the story about *you two* that's got the worst bite. The 'cheating wife' narrative. That's the one sticking."

Seth stiffened.

"I'm not asking you to lie," Marshall said. "Just... maybe don't let them write the ending for you. Let her focus on clearing her name without having to bleed for things she didn't do."

Seth stared down at the town, his jaw tense. "You want me to say we're okay."

"I want you to have her back, at least until the smoke clears."

Seth didn't answer right away. His voice, when it came, was low.

"I don't know if I can have her back in the house, Marshall. Not yet. She's been staying with *him*—Elliot. That's not a detail the town made up."

Marshall raised an eyebrow. "She's not staying with Elliot."

Seth looked over, skeptical. "You sure about that?"

"She's been sleeping above Valley Vogue," Marshall said. "Kathryn set up a little apartment there years ago—tiny place, couch bed and a kitchenette. She made it for herself when she worked late during holiday seasons and didn't want to drive out to the house at midnight."

Seth's lips parted. "She's not with him?"

Marshall shook his head. "No. She's alone."

A long beat passed. Then Seth muttered, "Oh."

Marshall clapped him on the shoulder. "You ought to talk to her."

Seth nodded, finally. "Yeah. I guess I will."

"Might be a good idea," Marshall said. "For both of you."

Back in town, Elliot found Cassie in the alley behind the boutique again.

She was smoking.

It startled him more than the news.

"I didn't know you smoked," he said softly.

"I don't. Not really." She flicked the ash. "Just felt like ruining one more thing today."

He stepped closer. "Cass—"

"Don't," she said, cutting him off. "Don't tell me it'll blow over. Don't tell me it'll be okay."

"I wasn't going to."

She finally looked at him.

"What were you going to say?"

He hesitated. "That I believe you. Still."

Cassie exhaled a shaky breath. "That's a rare thing today."

"You told the truth before they dragged it out of you. That matters."

She dropped the cigarette and crushed it under her heel. "Not enough."

Elliot moved toward her. "Look, if this is the end of the line—if you're walking away from everything—then fine. But do it on your terms. Not his."

She blinked back tears. "I'm so tired, Elliot."

"I know."

He reached out, gently wrapping his arms around her.

And for a few moments, she allowed herself to collapse into them.

Later that evening, Kathryn returned to the boutique to find a package waiting on the doorstep.

She picked it up warily—no return address, no markings.

Inside was a photograph.

It was Cassie again.

But this time, the image wasn't from her past.

It was from the present.

Cassie, outside Everbrew Café, her head on Elliot's shoulder.

And beneath it, written in thick black marker:

Ask yourself what else she hasn't told you.

Kathryn's hand trembled.

Whoever had sent it wanted one thing: to isolate Cassie.

To make her look like poison.

But Kathryn had made her decision.

She dropped the photo in the trash, locked the front door, and flipped the sign to *Closed*.

If the town wanted a show, they'd get one.

But it wouldn't be the one they expected.

9

Kathryn stood at the window of Valley Vogue, arms folded, staring out at the town she once believed she understood. Galen Valley wasn't exactly known for subtlety when it came to scandal. But this… this was different.

This was a slow, public dismantling of a woman who'd dared to be imperfect in a place that thrived on pretending everyone had it all together.

She watched as people walked by the boutique's window without looking in—people who normally waved. Stopped. Smiled. Now, they crossed the street like the building itself had become infected.

Cassie was still in the back room. Quiet. Withdrawing.

Kathryn was giving her space. For now.

But she knew the silence couldn't last much longer.

Cassie sat on the loveseat near the dressing rooms, knees tucked up beneath her. She hadn't cried today—not yet. But it was early.

She'd stared at herself in the mirror for ten minutes this morning, trying to decide who exactly she was now. She couldn't figure it out.

She wasn't the activist from Chicago anymore. She wasn't the quiet ranger's wife who made sourdough and pinned renovation ideas to boards she never used. And she definitely wasn't the boutique model with the "clean aesthetic" and Instagram-worthy candids.

She was none of them. And too much of all of them.

There was a knock on the back door.

She didn't move. Kathryn opened it.

Cassie couldn't hear the voice at first. But when the footsteps crossed the boutique floor—slow, deliberate, familiar—her breath caught.

Seth.

He appeared in the doorway to the backroom, still in his uniform, his eyes locked on hers like he was searching for a version of her he used to know.

"Hey," he said.

Cassie straightened slowly. "Hi."

Kathryn slipped out the side door, no words spoken.

Silence filled the room.

"I saw the article," he said finally. "And the follow-up."

Cassie looked down. "I figured."

"I should've said something earlier," he added. "I was angry. I *am* angry. But that's not why I came."

She lifted her gaze.

"I came because I still don't know how to stop loving you," he said quietly.

Tears stung her eyes.

"I don't know if we can fix this," he went on. "I don't know if I *want* to fix it. But I know I don't want to walk away without trying."

Cassie's throat tightened. "I don't deserve that."

"Maybe not," he said. "But I've made my own mistakes. Not asking the right questions. Pretending we were fine when we weren't. Not seeing how alone you were."

"I wasn't just alone," she whispered. "I was disappearing."

He stepped closer. "So let's find you again."

She wanted to believe him. She *ached* to believe him.

But the truth was still there—coiled like a storm.

"I'm not who I was when we met."

Seth's expression didn't change. "Neither am I."

There was a pause, heavy with everything unsaid.

"I, uh… I was wondering if you wanted to come back home," Seth said, his voice steady but quiet. "Not… not like that. Just… maybe stay in the guest room. It might calm down some of the noise. The rumors."

Cassie didn't answer right away.

"I know we're not there yet," Seth added, "and maybe we won't be. I just thought… maybe it'd take some of the pressure off."

Cassie looked at him, torn.

"It's not that I don't miss the house," she said. "I do. But staying here… it's the only thing that doesn't feel like pretending right now."

Seth's brow furrowed slightly. "Pretending?"

Cassie nodded. "When I was back at the house with you, I was smiling when I was falling apart inside. I wore that ring and played the part. I told myself it was right even when everything in me knew I wasn't ready for that life again. If I move back in just to make the town happy…" She looked down at her coffee mug. "Then I'm doing it all over again. I'm pretending. And I won't do that. Not to myself. And not to you."

Seth was quiet for a long moment.

Then he stood, walked over to her, and gently kissed her forehead.

"I get it," he said softly. "More than you know."

And with that, he turned and left the boutique.

Cassie sat in silence for a while after the door closed behind him—equal parts relief and heartbreak flooding her chest.

Because this time, the hardest part wasn't the distance between them.

It was knowing they were finally telling the truth.

Elliot stood at the edge of the high school parking lot, watching students file out for the day, their faces lit by the glow of screens and speculation.

He'd heard the whispers. The questions. Some students had seen the article. Others had watched their parents scroll furiously at dinner tables, muttering Cassie's name like it was a slur.

He knew what was coming.

He was next.

Sure enough, when he returned to his classroom, a note was waiting for him on his desk.

Elliot—please see me after school tomorrow. Principal Sweeney.

No explanation. None needed.

The board had been called.

That evening, Cassie walked to Everbrew Café. Alone.

She needed to reclaim something. A space. A moment. A choice.

She ordered her latte from the same barista who used to remember her drink. The girl didn't smile this time. Just rang her up, then disappeared into the back.

Cassie sat at the table near the window—the same one from that first conversation with Elliot—and stared out at the street.

It was the same view. But the town had changed.

Or maybe she had.

She pulled her phone from her bag and opened her email. There it was.

RE: National Media Inquiry – CNN/NBC Interested in Full Story. Please confirm interview availability.

Her finger hovered over the screen.

It would be so easy to step fully into the spotlight. To lean into it. Control it.

But she didn't want to be a symbol anymore.

She just wanted to be free.

Cassie deleted the email.

She walked back to the apartment slowly, feet aching, mind swirling.

As she turned down the street toward Kathryn's, she saw a figure waiting near the boutique steps.

Devon.

He clapped slowly as she approached.

"Well done," he said. "You made yourself a martyr."

"Leave."

"You're trending again," he smirked. "You should thank me."

She stood tall, jaw clenched. "I'm not afraid of you."

"Oh, you should be," he said, stepping closer. "Because if you think this is the worst I can do, you haven't been paying attention."

Cassie didn't speak. Didn't flinch.

She just looked him dead in the eye and said, "Do it."

Devon blinked. "Excuse me?"

"Leak whatever's left. Go ahead. But I'm done letting you hold the past over me."

He studied her—waiting for the cracks.

There were none.

He scoffed. "You always were good at grand exits."

And then he turned and walked away.

Inside, Kathryn waited in the kitchen with a cup of tea.

Cassie stepped in quietly, closed the door behind her, and said, "It's over."

Kathryn looked up. "Devon?"

Cassie nodded. "I told him to go ahead. I'm not running anymore."

Kathryn rose, crossed the room, and hugged her.

Cassie finally let herself cry.

Not from fear.

From release.

10

The news cycle slowed.

For two days, there were no new headlines. No fresh leaks. No anonymous threats. Devon had vanished as quickly as he arrived—like a storm that left only debris in its wake.

Cassie half-expected a second wave. Another ambush. But instead, there was… stillness.

And in that stillness, something remarkable happened.

People started talking.

Not just *about* her—but *to* her.

On Wednesday morning, a woman in her sixties came into *Valley Vogue* just after opening. Cassie had been steaming a rack of linen dresses when the bell above the door jingled.

The woman paused inside the doorway, her fingers curled tightly around her purse strap. Cassie recognized her vaguely—one of the church ladies, someone who normally wouldn't offer more than a polite nod in passing.

"I read the article," the woman said.

Cassie tensed. "Okay."

There was a pause.

Then: "I was twenty-four when I ran from St. Louis. I had a fiancé, a life I thought I wanted… but I left everything behind. There were things I didn't tell anyone."

Cassie stared at her.

The woman gave a small, wry smile. "Don't let this town convince you they've all lived perfect lives. We're just better at hiding the mess."

She walked out without buying anything, but her words stayed long after the door closed.

By the weekend, a few more followed.

Small gestures. Quiet acknowledgments.

A folded note in the boutique mailbox that said, *"I see you. I don't judge you."*

A bouquet left anonymously on the back steps.

A text from a local teacher thanking her for speaking her truth.

Not everyone was supportive. The whispers still echoed in corners. But the venom had less bite now.

The story was no longer being told *about* her.

She was telling it herself.

And somehow, that changed everything.

The front windows of Valley Vogue bathed the boutique in soft natural light, and Cassie stood near the mannequin display, the hem of a gauzy spring dress swaying as Kathryn adjusted the camera on her phone.

"Okay, head slightly to the left—chin up a little," Kathryn said, squinting through the lens. "There. That's it."

Cassie exhaled a laugh. "You're starting to sound like Elliot."

"God forbid," Kathryn muttered, grinning. "Okay, now walk toward me slowly. I want some movement in the fabric."

Cassie took a few slow steps, the heels of her boots clicking on the hardwood floor, the smile on her face finally feeling... real.

After the last shutter click, Kathryn lowered the phone and studied her.

"You know," she said gently, "you're starting to get that spark back."

Cassie raised an eyebrow, cheeks flushed from the impromptu shoot. "Spark?"

"Yeah. That shine in your eyes. It left for a while. But it's coming back." Kathryn reached into her purse and pulled out a clip to tame a wind-blown piece of Cassie's hair. "Now tell me—how are you really doing?"

Cassie hesitated.

Kathryn stepped closer. "I mean it. Don't smile. Don't dodge. No press-version of the truth. Just... talk to me. Tell me everything you're feeling."

Cassie sat on the edge of the display table and let her shoulders drop.

"I feel like I'm holding pieces of ten different lives," she said slowly. "There's the version of me that was married. The one who ran. The one who came back. The one who kissed Elliot. The one who nearly got swallowed by Chicago. And now there's this... version that some people suddenly connect to."

Kathryn nodded but didn't interrupt.

"I don't know which version is *me*," Cassie continued. "Or if all of them are. Or none of them."

Silence.

Then Kathryn gently reached out and took her hand.

"You're the one who stayed," she said. "Even when you could've run again. That's the version I see."

Cassie blinked, fighting back the emotion rising behind her eyes.

"I'm scared," she whispered.

"I know," Kathryn said. "But scared doesn't mean weak. It means you're smart enough to understand the risk."

Cassie let herself be still for a moment, soaking in the safety of it.

Then, a quiet smile broke across her lips.

"Thank you," she said. "For seeing me. Even when I don't."

"Always," Kathryn said. "Now let's post these photos and remind the ladies of Galen Valley that this boutique can still make them the best-dressed woman in town."

Elliot stepped into the principal's office just before noon on Thursday, his pulse drumming behind his ears.

Principal Sweeney gestured for him to sit. "Elliot. You know why you're here."

"Because of Cassie Dixon," he said evenly.

"Yes. And because the school board is concerned."

"Concerned about what?" Elliot asked. "That I care about someone who lives in town? Someone who told the truth when it would've been easier to lie?"

Principal Sweeney leaned forward. "They're worried about *perception*. About boundaries. About influence."

"I haven't broken any rules."

"No. But perception *is* part of our responsibility."

Elliot stayed silent.

Sweeney continued, "The board is placing you on temporary administrative leave while they investigate. Standard procedure."

"For being honest?" Elliot asked, unable to keep the bitterness from his voice.

"For getting involved in a high-profile controversy," Sweeney replied. "You'll continue to be paid. But we ask that you keep a low profile."

Elliot stood. "Low profile's never really been my thing."

That night, he knocked on the back door of the boutique after closing. Cassie answered, barefoot and in sweatpants, her hair tied up, eyes tired but warm.

"I got benched," he said simply.

"I'm so sorry," she breathed. "This is because of *me*."

"No," he said. "This is because Galen Valley still thinks appearances matter more than people."

She led him inside, and they sat in the small kitchenette.

"I don't regret it," he added. "Any of it."

Cassie looked at him, eyes glassy. "I do."

His chest tightened. "You regret *me*?"

"No," she whispered. "I regret what it cost you."

Elliot stayed seated on the edge of the worn couch, one hand resting loosely on his knee, the other gripping the back of his neck. Cassie stood by the small kitchen counter, arms folded, eyes distant.

"I never wanted to drag you into this," she said, her voice low. "I never thought we'd… cross a line. And now you're on administrative leave. Because of me."

He looked over at her, brow furrowed with a tenderness that made her stomach twist.

"I don't care about the leave," he said.

"But I do," she snapped softly, turning toward him. "Elliot, this is your *career*. Your livelihood. You built a reputation at that school."

He leaned back slightly, voice calm. "And maybe it's time for something else."

She blinked. "What?"

"I've been burned out for years, Cass," he admitted. "Hiding it. Smiling through rehearsals. Fighting with the board over every budget cut, every outdated policy. Meeting you didn't ruin anything. If anything, it reminded me how much I've been *sleepwalking* through my life."

Cassie crossed the room, standing in front of him now.

"You can't say that," she said. "Not when it might cost you everything. Not because of me."

He looked up at her, a quiet fire behind his words.

"Meeting you has been the best thing to happen to me in years. I don't regret caring for someone during a time when they were unraveling. That's not a scandal. That's *human*. If the school board can't see the difference, then maybe I don't need to be in that school anymore."

Cassie sank onto the couch beside him, heart racing. "But what will you do?"

Elliot shrugged. "Maybe pivot. Theater's not limited to high school stages. Maybe I direct again. Maybe I leave town. Maybe… things happen for a reason."

She looked at him, eyes wide and filled with tears she didn't want to fall.

"Don't give things up because of me."

"I'm not," he said, brushing her hand with his. "I'm giving things up because *they stopped being right for me.* And you helped me realize that."

Cassie leaned her head against his shoulder, the weight of it all pressing against her—but for the first time, not crushing.

And in the silence that followed, she let herself believe… maybe some endings were just the beginning of something more honest.

The next morning, Cassie found Seth waiting by the boutique steps, leaning against his truck with a cardboard cup of coffee in hand.

She approached slowly, uncertain. "Morning."

He held out the cup.

She took it.

"Elliot told me what happened," Seth said.

Cassie winced. "It's my fault."

"No," he said. "It's mine."

She looked up.

"I let you carry everything alone for so long," he said. "And I told myself it was because you were closed off. But really, I didn't *want* to see it. Because if I did, I'd have to admit we were already breaking."

Cassie swallowed hard. "So what now?"

Seth hesitated. "I don't have an answer. But I think… maybe we start by admitting it wasn't perfect. And then decide if we still want to try anyway."

Cassie blinked back emotion. "You still want to try?"

"I want to know if there's still something worth saving," he said. "But only if you want that too."

Cassie stared down at the coffee cup.

Warm. Familiar. Honest.

"I don't know what I want yet," she admitted.

"Then start there," Seth said gently. "Start with truth."

That night, Cassie walked to the overlook above the valley alone. The sky was streaked with lavender and gold, and below her, the town shimmered like a postcard.

Galen Valley had not forgiven her.

Not fully.

But it had begun, slowly, to *see* her.

And that was more than she'd ever dared hope for.

11

The boutique felt different now.

Lighter.

Kathryn noticed it too. She moved through the racks of linen skirts and soft knits with renewed energy, humming under her breath as she adjusted a mannequin's scarf.

Cassie was behind the counter, sorting through a fresh shipment of accessories. For the first time in weeks, her thoughts weren't filled with headlines, whispers, or fear.

The storm hadn't passed. Not entirely. But the worst of it, she hoped, had already hit.

Kathryn emerged from the back with a folder in hand. "You have a visitor."

Cassie looked up.

"Margaret Holloway," Kathryn added. "And she's got that look that means business."

They sat together in the boutique's fitting lounge, the familiar smell of lavender sachets and wood polish surrounding them.

Margaret handed Cassie a printout.

Cassie scanned the page: a call for guest contributors from a regional digital publication. Lifestyle. Small-town life. Human-interest stories.

"They want *me* to write?" she asked, eyebrows lifting.

Margaret nodded. "I pitched you. And they're interested."

"I'm not a writer."

"You're a *storyteller*," Margaret said. "And right now, there are people who need your voice. People who don't fit neatly into Galen Valley's boxes. You survived a public unraveling and didn't run."

"I almost did."

"But you didn't. That matters."

Cassie sat back, still processing. "I don't even know what I'd write about."

"Start with truth," Margaret said. "That's what brought people around. That's what *matters*."

That evening, Cassie took her laptop to the small kitchen table in the apartment, the tea kettle whistling softly behind her.

She stared at the blank screen, hands trembling over the keys.

And then she typed.

Galen Valley taught me what it feels like to be both invisible and under a microscope...

The words came faster than she expected.

Her fingers kept moving.

For the first time in months, the story belonged to *her*.

Elliot called just after ten.

"I heard about the article opportunity," he said.

"Margaret," Cassie replied with a small smile. "She's a puppet master."

"I'm proud of you."

Cassie exhaled softly. "I don't know what I'm doing."

"You're showing up," he said. "That's more than most."

There was silence for a moment, and then Cassie asked the question that had been sitting on her tongue for days.

"What do you want from me, Elliot?"

He didn't hesitate. "I want what's real."

She closed her eyes. "I don't know if I can give that to anyone right now."

The article went live two days later.

It was titled: *"After the Storm: What I Learned from Falling Apart in a Town That Pretends It Doesn't."*

The response was swift—and largely supportive.

The Galen Gazette republished it. A podcast invited her on as a guest. Even a small publishing house reached out to discuss future submissions.

Cassie wasn't sure how to process any of it.

So she didn't.

She just kept writing.

On Saturday morning, she returned to the house she hadn't stepped foot in for nearly three weeks.

Seth had mowed the lawn. Trimmed the hedges. Hung the hummingbird feeder back up on the porch.

He opened the door before she could knock.

"I'm not here to move back in," she said quickly. "I just... needed to see it."

He nodded. "You can come in, if you want."

She stepped inside.

The living room was exactly as she left it—except for the folded quilt on the back of the couch. The scent of cedar and old books still hung in the air.

"This house doesn't feel like mine anymore," she said, voice soft.

"It always felt like ours to me," he replied.

She turned to face him. "I don't know what that means anymore."

Seth studied her. "Can I show you something?"

She nodded.

He led her to the garage, flicked on the light.

A workbench was set up in the corner, and on top of it—a wooden sign. Half-carved. Her name.

Cassie blinked. "What is this?"

"I started it before everything fell apart," he said. "I wanted to hang it over the garden. Your space. You never really had one here."

Cassie reached out and touched the grooves of the letters. Her throat tightened.

"I want you to have space now," Seth said. "Not just in the house. In *us.*"

She nodded. Slowly. "I don't know what that looks like yet."

"Then we figure it out together."

That night, as she sat in bed with her laptop and a mug of sleepytime tea, a notification pinged in her inbox.

One message.

Subject line: *Hello again.*

The sender?

Natalie Oliver.

Cassie's breath caught in her throat.

Natalie.

The whistleblower.

The one person from Chicago who knew *everything.*

The email was short.

Cass—

Saw your article. Impressed. I'm in Charlotte now. There's something you need to know. Call me.

—N

Cassie stared at the screen, heart pounding.

Whatever she thought had been left in the past… wasn't.

12

Cassie sat at the kitchen table, the email from Natalie still open on her laptop, her tea gone cold beside it.

She hadn't thought of Natalie Oliver in years—not really. After everything with the nonprofit imploded, Natalie had vanished into the shadows with the rest of it. Cassie assumed she'd started over. New job. New city. New identity, maybe.

She never imagined Natalie would reach out.

Certainly not now. Not when Cassie's life was finally, cautiously, rebuilding itself.

She reread the message three times before grabbing her phone.

She didn't text.

She called.

Natalie answered on the second ring.

"Cass."

Her voice was the same—crisp, guarded, but unmistakably her.

"Hi," Cassie said, her own voice rasping with nerves. "I got your email."

"I figured you would. I didn't expect you to actually call."

"I almost didn't."

"Why did you?"

Cassie hesitated. "Because I need to know what you meant. You said there's something I need to know."

There was silence on the other end. Then a sigh.

"I'm coming to Galen Valley," Natalie said.

Cassie sat up straighter. "You're what?"

"I'll be there Sunday. I'll explain everything then. Just... be ready."

And with that, Natalie hung up.

Cassie stared at the phone in her hand, heart hammering.

Be ready?

Ready for *what*?

On Sunday, the sky over Galen Valley was heavy and gray, the kind of sky that made everything feel like it was holding its breath.

Cassie stood at the front window of Valley Vogue, arms folded tight against her chest as the town moved slowly outside.

Kathryn noticed her pacing and set down her mug of chai. "You're sure about this?"

"No," Cassie admitted. "But she's already on her way."

"Do you want me here?"

Cassie shook her head. "This isn't a boutique conversation."

Kathryn nodded and squeezed her arm. "Just remember—you're not the girl you were back then."

"I don't know who I am right now."

"Yes, you do," Kathryn said. "You're just afraid to trust her."

Natalie arrived at exactly one o'clock.

Cassie opened the back door before she had a chance to knock.

Natalie stood in the doorway in a black trench coat, her hair shorter than Cassie remembered, and a canvas bag slung over one shoulder.

For a moment, they just stared at each other.

Then Natalie smiled—faint, guarded.

"I brought coffee."

Cassie stepped aside.

They sat in the backroom of the boutique, two coffees between them, tension hanging in the air like storm clouds.

"I saw the article," Natalie said finally. "It was brave."

"It was overdue."

"Still," Natalie said, "brave."

Cassie took a slow breath. "Why are you here?"

Natalie reached into her bag and pulled out a manila folder. She slid it across the table.

"Devon's not done."

Cassie froze. "What?"

"He's been shopping around a bigger story. Not about you—about the whole operation. The nonprofit. The off-book donations. And he's using you as bait."

"Why?"

"Because you're the one who walked away clean," Natalie said. "And now you're visible again. People trust you. So if he can drag you back in, *everything* explodes."

Cassie opened the folder.

Inside were copies of internal memos, banking statements, even a redacted affidavit—signed just a few weeks ago.

Cassie's stomach dropped. "Who gave this to you?"

"I have friends in places Devon doesn't know about," Natalie said. "But I came to you because if this goes public, they'll come after *both* of us."

Cassie stared at the paperwork. "So what do you want from me?"

"Help me stop it."

Cassie looked up. "How?"

"Go on the record. But not about you—about *him.* Flip the narrative. Be the voice again, before Devon spins you back into the villain."

Cassie leaned back in her chair, the weight of the last few months suddenly crashing down on her shoulders.

"I can't survive another war, Natalie."

"You already did," Natalie said softly. "Now help me finish it."

That evening, Cassie walked down the quiet streets of Galen Valley alone.

She felt cooped up. In the apartment. In life.

She walked to the overlook above the valley, just as the first drops of rain began to fall.

Natalie's words played on repeat in her head.

Now help me finish it.

She thought about the girl she used to be.

The one who believed in justice so fiercely that she broke things trying to reach it.

She'd spent so long trying to forget that girl.

Now she wasn't sure she could afford to.

Because the truth was, that girl wasn't just part of her story.

She *was* the story.

And maybe it was time to stop running from her—and start listening.

13

Cassie didn't sleep.

She lay on the couch in the apartment, staring at the ceiling while the storm outside swept through the valley, rattling window panes and pelting the balcony with rain.

Natalie's folder sat on the kitchen table, its manila edges curling slightly under the humidity.

Cassie had read every page. Twice.

Each line dragged her deeper into memories she'd tried so hard to repress—late-night strategy sessions with Devon and Natalie, cold sweats before board meetings, the moment she realized they'd gone too far.

And then the aftermath.

The fear.

The headlines.

The silence.

She hadn't felt this kind of pressure since she left Chicago.

But now, something was different.

She wasn't hiding.

Not anymore.

By mid-afternoon, the rain had passed and a low fog hung over the hills like a veil. Galen Valley felt muted, as if the town itself were holding its breath again.

Cassie sat in the boutique with her laptop open, cursor blinking on a blank document.

A draft statement. For the press.

She hadn't told Kathryn yet. Or Elliot. Or Seth.

Not because she didn't trust them.

But because once the words were written, once they were sent...

There'd be no turning back.

She began to type.

The next morning, Elliot stood in the front office of Galen Valley High, freshly shaven, button-down crisp, trying to look as composed as possible despite the nausea swirling in his gut.

Principal Sweeney waved him into the conference room where two school board members waited, folders stacked neatly in front of them like weapons.

"Mr. Rhodes," the woman on the left began, "we appreciate your cooperation during this internal review."

He nodded. "I've done nothing wrong."

"The board understands there was no breach of professional conduct inside the school," she said. "But your relationship with Mrs. Dixon has created a considerable amount of public attention."

"She's not a student. She's not even affiliated with the school. She's a private citizen."

"Correct," the man interjected. "But your visibility as a public employee matters. Especially in a town like ours."

"Exactly," the woman added. "And the optics—your name being tied to a controversial figure—raises concerns. We've had parents call. We've had donors ask questions."

Elliot folded his hands on the table. "So what are you saying?"

"You can return to teaching," Principal Sweeney said, "but we strongly recommend you maintain distance from Mrs. Dixon—at least publicly."

Elliot leaned back, heart racing.

"So if I lie about who I care about and pretend they don't exist in public, then I can keep my job."

Sweeney's eyes narrowed. "That's not what we said."

"It's what you meant," Elliot replied. He stood. "You want to manage perception? Fine. Do it with someone else because I refuse to live a life of lies."

And with that, he walked out.

Cassie was still typing when her phone buzzed. It was a text from Seth.

You free for dinner tonight? No pressure. Just want to talk.

She stared at the screen for a long moment before responding.

Yes. 6?

Seth responded:

I'll cook.

She smiled then sent:

And I'll listen.

That evening, she returned to the house on Wren Street.

Seth greeted her in a soft gray henley, barefoot, the scent of roasted vegetables and garlic filling the space. The table was already set.

Cassie blinked. "This feels... normal."

Seth shrugged. "I figured we could try on 'normal' for a night. See how it fits."

They ate in silence for a while—comfortable, quiet.

Then Seth set his fork down.

"I saw her," he said.

Cassie looked up. "Natalie?"

He nodded. "She came into the station. Said she was visiting a friend."

"More like delivering a warning."

He studied her face. "She told me you might go public again. Bigger this time."

Cassie swallowed. "I'm writing the statement."

Seth nodded slowly. "Are you sure?"

"No," she admitted. "But I'm tired of being chased by my past. I want to confront it on *my* terms."

He leaned forward, eyes steady. "Then you won't do it alone."

Her breath caught. "You'd support me?"

"I may not understand all of it," he said. "But I know who you are now. And I'd rather stand beside the version of you that tells the truth—even when it's messy—than live with someone who's pretending."

Later that night, Elliot met Cassie outside the overlook trail, headlights casting shadows through the trees.

"You heard?" she asked.

He nodded. "Word travels fast when it's about you."

"Are you mad?"

He gave a small laugh. "I just told the school board I'd rather lose my job than pretend you don't exist."

Her eyes widened. "You did what?"

"They wanted me to play it safe. I'm not interested."

She stepped closer. "This won't be easy."

"Nothing worth it ever is."

He reached for her hand, and she let him take it.

"I'm scared," she whispered.

"So am I," he said.

They stood in silence, watching the stars blink out one by one behind drifting clouds.

Together.

The boutique had gone still hours ago. No creaking floors, no traffic outside—just the occasional soft groan of old wood settling as

Cassie lay on the small couch bed upstairs, the ceiling casting faint shadows above her.

She'd changed into a worn T-shirt and leggings but hadn't moved beneath the covers. Her eyes were open, lost in thought.

Dinner with Seth had been… warm.

Simple.

Familiar in a way that made her ache. They'd laughed. Talked about the town, about her writing, even about mundane things like the best place to get burgers on the edge of Pinecrest County. It had felt—if only briefly—like home again.

And then there was Elliot.

She'd met him afterwards, just for a few minutes. A quiet moment at the overlook, where their hands had found each other without even trying.

She closed her eyes.

How can a heart stretch so far and still feel whole?

Seth completed her in some ways. Their history. Their shared silences.

But in the ways Seth couldn't reach her—Elliot was there.

Elliot brought out the Cassie who wanted to escape, explore, *breathe.*

Still, even in the quiet—

A guilt gnawed at her.

Even separated, she and Seth were still married. Their vows, though bruised and bent, remained unbroken. And Cassie took that seriously. She always had.

Lying to herself about it wouldn't make the feelings go away.

But facing them?

She didn't know if she was strong enough for that yet.

This evening with Seth had felt so natural. So *right.*

And yet… so did holding Elliot's hands.

Cassie rolled onto her side, eyes welling but refusing to spill.

The worst part wasn't loving them both.

The worst part was realizing that in choosing one—
She might have to lose a part of herself either way.

14

Cassie hit "Send" on the email at 7:42 a.m.

Her open letter to the media was attached as a PDF, her statement short, direct, and final.

It had taken her three sleepless nights and two panic attacks to write it. Margaret Holloway reviewed it. Kathryn proofed it. Natalie added one strategic paragraph and then removed it again, saying, "No. This needs to be just *you*."

So it was.

I was complicit. Not criminal. But I was a coward.

I let others speak louder because I was afraid of what telling the truth would cost me.

Now I understand: silence costs more.

This is me. This is my story. And I won't let anyone else weaponize it again.*

—Cassie Dixon

By noon, it was everywhere.

Blogs. Facebook. National outlets. The same publication that had published Devon's leak posted an update: *"Cassie Dixon Speaks Out—In Her Own Words."*

The narrative shifted again. But this time, Cassie was in control of the steering wheel.

The internet was a double-edged sword.

Half the responses called her brave. Half called her manipulative. Some wanted more dirt. Others asked how to help.

And in Galen Valley?

The response was swift—and complicated.

Kathryn came into the back office of the boutique mid-afternoon, her phone buzzing nonstop.

"We've had seventeen cancellations for the weekend shoot," she said. "But we've also gotten six new bookings from people saying they came because of *you.*"

Cassie didn't know how to feel.

"That's… a strange balance."

"Welcome to the new age," Kathryn said. "You either scare people off, or you pull them in."

Cassie set down her tea. "I didn't do it to win fans."

"I know," Kathryn said. "And that's exactly why it's working."

At the ranger station, Seth stood at his desk with the letter printed and folded in his coat pocket.

He didn't need to read it again.

He'd read it five times already.

But he liked having it on him—like a talisman. A reminder that his wife—estranged or not—was not running anymore. That meant something to him.

Still, the radio calls crackled with tension.

Some in the law enforcement community supported her. Others muttered things under their breath.

"Guess the sheriff's wife is hiring radicals now," one of them said on an open channel, forgetting—or not caring—that Seth could hear.

Seth picked up the mic.

"This is Ranger Dixon," he said, voice like steel. "And if anyone's got a problem with someone telling the truth, maybe it's time to look in the mirror."

There was silence after that.

The kind that said everything.

At the high school, Elliot arrived to find two school board members waiting for him in the auditorium.

Again. He had walked out on them but they had not officially fired him....yet.

Principal Sweeney stood in the background, unreadable.

"We've reviewed your social media," one of them began.

"Is that even legal?" Elliot asked.

"You're a public educator. Public presence comes with it."

Elliot folded his arms. "Let me guess—you're going to ask me one more time to disassociate."

"We're asking you to stop making *her* your platform."

"She's not a platform," he said coldly. "She's a person. And she's telling the truth."

"There are parents threatening to pull students. Sponsors expressing concern. This goes beyond your personal life now."

Elliot looked between them.

"I quit."

The words shocked even him as they fell from his mouth.

"I'm not going to sit in a building full of cowards who care more about noise than about character."

He grabbed his messenger bag and walked out of the auditorium before anyone could respond.

Cassie was folding scarves in the boutique when he arrived.

"I quit," Elliot said, out of breath.

She looked up. "You what?"

"I quit the school. Or, I guess I got *provoked* into quitting. Either way—"

"Elliot, you didn't have to do that for me."

"I didn't," he said. "I did it for *me.* I can't teach students about integrity and then turn around and hide from the truth."

He exhaled. "Besides, I've been thinking about going back to theater. Real theater. Writing. Directing."

Cassie stepped forward. "You'd leave Galen Valley?"

"Maybe not forever. But maybe long enough to figure out who I am when I'm not hiding either."

Cassie reached for his hand. "We're both changing, aren't we?"

"I think we already did," he said. "Now we're just catching up to it."

That night, someone spray-painted the words *WIFE'S A LIAR* on the side of Seth's truck.

Cassie saw it when she pulled into the driveway to pick up a few things.

She stood staring at it until Seth came out with a bucket and a scrub brush.

"You don't have to—" she began.

"I know," he said. "But I want to."

They scrubbed in silence. Together.

When they finished, he leaned against the truck, breathing heavily.

"This town's getting louder," he said.

Cassie nodded. "But I'm not afraid of the noise anymore."

"Me neither."

They didn't kiss.

They didn't hold hands.

But something passed between them—steady, unspoken.

Maybe not love.

But something like understanding.

Later that night, Cassie opened her inbox.

Another message.

Mrs. Dixon—We'd like to invite you to speak at our regional journalism ethics panel this fall. We believe your voice matters.

—Atlantic Writers Coalition

Cassie sat back in her chair.

She didn't respond right away.

She just stared at the message and smiled.

Because for the first time in a long, long time…

Her voice mattered.

The boutique was quiet, the morning sun just beginning to spill through the front windows as Kathryn unlocked the door and carried in two paper coffee cups from the café.

Cassie was already inside, perched on the edge of the checkout counter, a stack of mail beside her but untouched.

Kathryn handed her a coffee. "You're up early."

Cassie took the cup with a faint smile. "Didn't sleep much."

Kathryn narrowed her eyes as she set down her bag. "Something happen?"

Cassie hesitated, then pulled a piece of paper from her pocket and held it out.

Kathryn opened it, scanned it.

Her eyes lit up. "Cassie! The Atlantic Writers Coalition! This is *huge.* Do you know how many people would kill for this kind of platform?"

"I know," Cassie said softly.

Kathryn studied her. "But you're not acting like someone who just got invited to sit at the table with national journalists."

Cassie looked down, wrapping both hands around her coffee.

"I got the email after the incident with Seth's truck," she said.

Kathryn's brows lifted.

"I stopped by the house to grab a few things," Cassie continued. "His truck had been vandalized, the words *WIFE'S A LIAR* spray-painted on it."

"And?"

"We started cleaning it off–together." Cassie exhaled. "Being near him again—it pulled something in me. The pendulum started swinging... and I'm afraid of where it might land."

Kathryn moved closer, quiet now.

"I care about Elliot," Cassie whispered. "More than I ever meant to. But Seth... he knows me in a different way. He's woven into the bones of my life."

"And now?" Kathryn asked.

"I don't know." Cassie's voice cracked. "Elliot quit his job because of me. And now he's just waiting for me to decide who I am and where I stand, and I'm standing here doing *nothing*."

She looked up, eyes glassy.

"It's all a complete mess, and it's *my* fault. I feel—" she shook her head "—I feel toxic."

Kathryn gently took the coffee from her hands and set it down.

"Cassie," she said firmly, "you are not toxic."

"You don't know what it's like to be the one who breaks things just by being unsure."

"Oh, honey." Kathryn sat beside her on the counter, their shoulders touching. "I may not have your exact story, but trust me—I know what it's like to feel like you're the storm instead of the sky."

Cassie blinked at her, lips parting slightly.

"But you're *not* the storm," Kathryn added. "You're the anchor. And people just keep crashing into you."

Cassie smiled weakly, a tear slipping down her cheek.

"You'll figure this out," Kathryn said. "And I'll be here for every messy step of it. But don't you dare believe for a second that love—your love—makes you poison."

Cassie nodded, wiped her cheek, and leaned into the moment.

"I don't know what I did to deserve you," she whispered.

Kathryn squeezed her hand. "You survived. You stayed. That's enough."

15

Cassie stood at the edge of the overlook, the same place she'd returned to again and again these past few months.

Below, Galen Valley shimmered in the soft morning light—its familiar rooftops, its winding streets, its church spires and town square all cloaked in the kind of peace that looked good on postcards but rarely extended to the people living in its corners.

Behind her, a new world was calling.

The email from the Atlantic Writers Coalition hadn't been the only offer.

A nonprofit in Charlotte reached out, asking her to consider coming on as a part-time media ethics advisor. A local podcast invited her to co-host a limited series about public redemption stories. An editor wanted her to turn her essays into a memoir.

And for the first time in years, Cassie didn't feel small when she considered saying yes.

But she didn't feel ready to say no, either.

Elliot sat on the porch of his rental cabin, a small U-Haul trailer hitched behind his car, the theater script he'd been tinkering with for three years finally finished and printed in a folder beside him.

He wasn't leaving for good.

But he was leaving long enough to put space between what had happened here and whatever came next.

At the ranger station, Seth was standing over a map of the national forest when Marshall came in, jaw tight.

"We've got a situation," Marshall said.

"What kind?"

"Missing person."

Seth looked up sharply.

"College student. Backpacker. Supposed to check in at Wren Hollow yesterday. Never showed. Car's still parked at the trailhead."

"Locals?"

"No. Out-of-towner. But here's where it gets complicated." Marshall unfolded a crumpled paper. "This flyer showed up at the station this morning."

It was a black-and-white printout.

A screenshot of Cassie's face from the media fallout—her name in bold, the word *Manipulator* scrawled underneath.

Seth's blood ran cold. "Someone's trying to stir the pot."

Marshall nodded. "And if this missing kid's story gets tied to you or Cassie—even loosely—it's going to rip the wound wide open again."

Seth looked away. "We'll find him."

"Yeah," Marshall said. "But let's make sure we find him *before* someone else finds a new story to tell."

Cassie was packing for Charlotte when Kathryn stopped by the apartment with a small box wrapped in twine.

"What's this?" Cassie asked.

"A gift. For the next chapter," Kathryn said, smiling.

Inside was a necklace.

A tiny, gold pine tree charm.

"I thought you might want to take a piece of the valley with you," she said.

Cassie's throat tightened. "I haven't said I'm leaving yet, it's just an interview."

"No," Kathryn said. "But you're ready to."

Cassie sat down slowly, her mind swirling.

"Do you ever regret staying?" she asked. "Staying in Galen Valley?"

Kathryn paused. "Sometimes. But then I remember—this town may not *deserve* every part of you. But it *needs* people like you to change it."

Cassie smiled faintly. "You sound like Margaret."

"I've been listening."

Cassie took a slow sip of water as Kathryn sat on the couch next to her, a warm smirk tugging at the corners of her lipstick-lined mouth.

"You know," Kathryn said, folding one leg over the other, "when I moved here from New York, I thought I'd made the biggest mistake of my life."

Cassie blinked. "You're from the city?"

Kathryn nodded, her eyes glinting with fondness and a touch of mischief. "Born in Queens, raised on bagels and bluntness. I met Marshall at a friend's engagement party upstate. He was visiting family and stood out like a sore thumb—all flannel and Southern drawl. I couldn't tell if he was lost or just *charming*. Turns out, it was both."

Cassie chuckled softly.

"We fell fast. I moved here after six months, got married in nine. And then the campaign started."

"For sheriff?"

"Mhmm," Kathryn said. "And suddenly, I wasn't just Marshall's wife. I was supposed to be his image. Supportive, clean-cut, respectable—but not too flashy." She raised her eyebrows pointedly. "And you *know* how well that went over."

"I can imagine," Cassie said, smiling.

"I had women in the market whispering behind my back because I wore heels to the bakery. One woman told me I'd 'give the wrong impression' dressing like I was headed to the Upper East Side instead of church."

Cassie scoffed. "You're kidding."

"I wish I were." Kathryn leaned forward. "But here's the twist—I kept showing up. Every day during that campaign, I walked this town in pencil skirts, perfect lipstick, and heels that made no sense for gravel driveways. I shook hands, kissed babies, and smiled through gritted teeth."

She paused, eyes softening.

"And then something weird happened. The women who once rolled their eyes started pulling me aside. Asking where I got my boots. How I did my makeup. If I could help them pick something to wear to their daughter's wedding or their husband's promotion dinner."

Cassie leaned in, fascinated.

"That's when it hit me. These women weren't judging me. They just *didn't know how to be seen.* This town didn't give them space to feel beautiful. Not really. So I decided to create one."

"Valley Vogue," Cassie whispered.

"Valley Vogue," Kathryn confirmed. "Marshall helped me lease this building. We painted it ourselves and ate pizza off a toolbox the night before it opened. That was the best decision we ever made together. He's got his law enforcement and his hunting cabin in the woods—God help me—and I have *this.*"

She glanced around the apartment, the walls were filled with pencil sketches of dresses and glamorous magazine covers, there was a display dress form in the corner of the room with a fur stole and layers of necklaces on it.

"It works," she said. "It keeps us happy."

Cassie's chest warmed.

"Thank you for telling me that," she said softly.

Kathryn smiled, eyes sparkling. "Every woman who's ever come through Valley Vogue's doors has a story, Cass. You're just the first one who showed up already dressed for battle."

Later that afternoon, Cassie drove to the ranger station. Seth was just coming in from the trail—his jacket damp, his boots muddy.

"You look like hell," she said softly.

"Long day," he replied. "Long month."

She stepped closer. "Marshall told me. About the missing hiker. And the flyer."

Seth nodded. "People still want a villain. They're just not sure who to settle on."

"I'm sorry."

"You don't need to apologize."

Cassie looked down. "I might leave. Charlotte's calling."

Seth studied her. "You should go."

Her head snapped up. "You think so?"

"I think you've been shrinking to fit here," he said. "And I want you to expand. Even if it means I don't get to be in the next version of your life."

Cassie's eyes stung.

"I'll always care about you," he added. "Even when we don't make sense."

She nodded. "You were my safe place."

"You were mine, too."

They stood in silence for a long moment, the past heavy between them.

Then Cassie kissed his cheek, whispered, "Thank you," and walked away.

That night, Elliot came by just before sunset.

His car was loaded. His trailer hitched. His eyes tired but hopeful.

Cassie met him in the alley behind Valley Vogue.

"No goodbyes," she said.

"No promises," he replied.

Just a look.

And then a quiet, gentle hug that said everything.
She watched him drive off, taillights fading into the dusk.
Not the end.
Just a new chapter.

Cassie returned inside, took a breath, and opened her laptop.
She began to write.
Not an essay.
Not a statement.
Not a defense.
A story.
The story.
For the first time—not about surviving the storm.
But about becoming the one who learned to dance in it.

16

The hum of the city was different.

In Charlotte, the air carried the low throb of traffic, coffee shops, and buskers strumming chords outside bookstores. It was a sharp contrast to Galen Valley's quiet rhythm—a reminder that Cassie Dixon had returned to a world that didn't know her as a scandal, a wife, or a cautionary tale.

Here, she was just a woman with a laptop and a voice still shaking off its fear. The interview went well, she found an affordable studio and so she decided to stay.

The nonprofit consulting gig was modest, remote, and slightly ironic—offering guidance on public transparency for the same kind of organizations that once buried her. But it paid well. And no one had yet recognized her in the café she'd claimed as her office.

Cassie was beginning to believe she might finally be in control.

Until her phone buzzed.

Seth Dixon.

She stared at the name for a long moment before answering.

"Hey."

"Cass," his voice was steady but tight. "Sorry to call out of nowhere, but something's come up."

"Are you okay?"

"Yeah. It's not about me," he said. "It's about the missing hiker."

Her stomach turned.

"Okay..."

"There's more to the story than we thought. You may want to come back."

"Why?"

"Because the guy had a folder full of articles about you. And Natalie. And Devon."

Cassie gripped the edge of the table. "Are you saying he was looking for me?"

"We don't know yet. But you showing up on a missing person's radar? That's not nothing."

The drive to Galen Valley felt shorter this time.

Familiar.

Like muscle memory wrapped in pine needles and gravel roads.

Cassie arrived late, pulling into the ranger station as a light mist settled over the valley. Seth met her on the steps, arms crossed, expression unreadable beneath his ball cap.

"You didn't have to come this fast," he said.

Cassie shrugged. "You called. I came."

They walked inside together. Marshall wasn't there—it was his day off—but one of his deputies handed Seth a sealed manila envelope and nodded toward the back.

Inside the conference room, Seth spread the contents across the table: printed screenshots, highlighted search histories, emails recovered from the hiker's cloud account.

One name stood out over and over again.

Cassie Dixon.

"What's his name and why was he looking for me?" she asked.

Seth pointed to one email: a draft. Unsigned. Never sent.

You don't know me, but I know what Devon Blake did. I think it's still happening. And I think you can help me stop it.

Cassie leaned back in her chair, pulse pounding.

"He thought I'd help him."

"Maybe. Or maybe he thought you'd lead him to the story he wanted. His name is Tyler Griggs."

Cassie looked up. "And now he's missing."

Seth didn't answer.

He didn't have to.

Cassie found herself back at the apartment again, the boutique dark and quiet after hours.

"I thought I was done being pulled back into this mess," she said.

Kathryn poured her a glass of wine. "Honey, the past doesn't have an expiration date."

Cassie swirled the glass. "He's missing and more than likely dead because he was chasing ghosts."

"Or because someone didn't want those ghosts dug up."

Cassie froze. "You think this is connected to Devon?"

"I think people with power don't like being exposed. And Tyler wasn't just some lost hiker. He was a threat to someone."

Cassie nodded slowly. "Then I need to figure out what he knew."

Kathryn sipped her wine. "Be careful. You might not like what you find."

Cassie poured the last of the wine into their glasses as Kathryn tucked her feet under her on the couch, her silk blouse slightly wrinkled from a long day but her presence as polished and comforting as ever.

"That poor kid," Kathryn said softly, swirling the red wine in her glass. "Wandering out there alone."

"I know," Cassie replied, settling into the opposite end of the couch.

They sat in silence for a few moments, sipping their wine, the boutique below them dark and still.

Then Kathryn turned to her.

"Can I ask you something?"

Cassie raised an eyebrow. "Since when do you ask?"

Kathryn smirked. "Fair. But I'm being serious."

"Go ahead."

"What happens after this? After the investigation. After the dust settles." She paused. "Do you go back to Charlotte? To the non-profit work?"

Cassie blinked, caught off guard. She hadn't let herself think that far ahead.

"I don't know," she said honestly. "It is important work. Meaningful. But... it doesn't feel like mine."

Kathryn looked at her quizzically. "What do you mean?"

Cassie shook her head. "Because that work is about making waves from a distance. But Galen Valley? This place makes me *show up* in the middle of the storm."

Kathryn studied her. "You sound like someone who's not just visiting anymore."

Cassie stared at her wine for a long moment. "I used to think this town was a cage. Now, I'm not so sure it isn't a second chance."

Kathryn smiled, warm and wise. "Then don't waste it looking backward."

Cassie clinked her glass gently against hers. "I won't."

They sipped again in companionable silence.

And for the first time in weeks, Cassie felt not just grounded—but quietly, stubbornly hopeful.

17

Cassie had barely slept.

She sat at the small table near the boutique's window, a legal pad filled with scribbled notes and printouts spread in front of her. Kathryn had opened early and hadn't asked too many questions—just set a cup of strong coffee in front of her and nodded.

Cassie tapped her pen against the table, eyes scanning Tyler Griggs' digital footprint.

There was nothing overt—no manifesto, no incriminating confessions—but what she *did* find were breadcrumbs.

His social media accounts had been quiet for months, but he followed a trail of accounts all orbiting the scandal she once tried to bury: investigative journalists, nonprofit watchdogs, and fringe blogs that still carried headlines with her name.

More concerning, though, was the string of messages he'd left unanswered in a Reddit thread titled:

"The Truth Behind the Whistleblowers No One Talks About."

Cassie hadn't been on Reddit in years. She clicked through carefully.

The username was @TylerG87, and his comments, though brief, made one thing clear: he believed there was more to the Devon Blake cover-up than anyone had publicly revealed. And he thought Cassie might be the missing link.

One thread sent chills down her spine.

@TylerG87: *"Cassie Dixon vanished into Galen Valley. That's not a coincidence. If you want to know who funded the cover-up, look where she ended up."*

Cassie stared at it for a long time.

She hadn't even heard about Galen Valley until she met Seth and this is where he had grown up and was stationed as a ranger. Nothing nefarious about it or so she thought. Now she wasn't so sure. She needed to talk to Seth.

Seth was already at the station when Cassie arrived, still wearing his trail gear, mud splashed up the sides of his boots. He looked up as she entered and gave a tired nod.

"I've been digging."

"So have I," she said, dropping a folder on his desk. "Tyler was following me long before he came here."

Seth opened the folder, flipping through the printouts. "This is… deeper than we thought."

"I think someone led him here. And I don't think he was just trying to *expose* me. I think he believed I could help him blow the whole thing open."

Seth leaned back in his chair, rubbing his temples. "And now he's dead."

Cassie nodded grimly. "Whoever brought him here might not have been looking for the truth. They were looking for *silence*."

Before Seth could respond, Deputy Ranger Justin Foster knocked on the door.

"You've got visitors," he said, eyeing Cassie. "Internal Affairs."

Seth's stomach dropped. "IA? What the hell for?"

Foster shrugged. "Said it's about the hiker."

Cassie's eyes widened. "You're being investigated?"

"Looks like it," Seth said, jaw clenched.

Foster gave a tight nod. "They want to speak with you. Alone."

Cassie stepped back, instinctively protective. "They think you had something to do with it?"

"I don't know," Seth said. "But when people want to distract from the truth, they go after the ones asking the wrong questions."

Elliot Rhodes sat on a bench outside a coffeehouse in Raleigh, his phone vibrating in his hand.

He'd tried not to check the Galen Valley gossip groups since he left. He'd promised himself he wouldn't look back, wouldn't get drawn in again.

But a message from Margaret Holloway had pulled him in anyway.

"You should call Cassie. Something's happening again."

Now, he scrolled through the same Reddit thread Cassie had seen. His heart sank.

People were speculating that Tyler Griggs' death was staged, that Galen Valley was some kind of secretive cover-up town, that Cassie was part of a bigger conspiracy.

He couldn't stay silent.

He pulled up Cassie's number and hit dial.

She answered on the first ring.

"Elliot?"

"I'm sorry," he said. "I told myself I wouldn't call. I just—Margaret messaged me. And then I saw the posts."

Cassie rubbed her forehead. "You saw the thread."

"I saw everything. I think you're being set up."

Her voice broke slightly. "They're investigating Seth."

"I can come back."

"No," she said quickly. "Don't. Not unless it gets worse."

"Cassie…"

She closed her eyes. "We're so close to the truth. If someone wants to shut me up, they're going to have to try a lot harder."

He exhaled. "Just promise me you won't do this alone."

"I won't," she said.

And this time, she meant it.

Later that night, as the fog rolled in and Cassie stood outside the back of the boutique for some fresh air, a small white envelope slid beneath the front door.

She picked it up cautiously.

There was no name. No stamp. Just two words written in small, neat handwriting:

"Dig deeper."

Inside was a photo.

A blurry image of two men—Devon Blake and someone Cassie didn't recognize—standing near a trailhead sign marked Wren Hollow.

The date stamp?

Two weeks before Tyler Griggs disappeared.

Cassie stared at it, heart pounding.

Devon had been back in Galen Valley.

And this time, she wouldn't be the one running.

18

Cassie stared at the photo long after the boutique had gone dark. She'd locked the doors. Drawn the shades. But the image burned behind her eyelids every time she blinked.

Devon.

Standing at the entrance to Wren Hollow, relaxed and unbothered. The man beside him wore a hood, his face obscured—but the body language was familiar. Comfortable. Like they were equals.

Accomplices.

She flipped the photo over.

No message. No signature.

Just that date—scrawled in pencil: 2/11.

Two weeks before Tyler vanished.

At the sheriff's office, Marshall Bowen was uncharacteristically silent as Cassie slid the photo across his desk the next morning. Seth sat beside her, arms crossed, unreadable.

"I know what you're thinking," she said. "But I didn't know he was back in Galen Valley."

"I don't think you brought him here," Marshall said. "But I think someone wants you to believe you did."

He tapped the photo. "You recognize the man with him?"

Cassie shook her head. "Not exactly. But the build… the posture. It reminds me of someone."

Seth leaned forward. "There's something else."

He pulled a manila envelope from his coat pocket and opened it.

"Trail cam footage. One of our old forest units we forgot was still live. It's from the same day. And look who shows up about twenty minutes after this photo was taken."

He turned the screen on his laptop, inserted the flash drive and played the video.

There, stepping cautiously into the edge of the frame, was a lone figure.

Tyler Griggs.

Cassie's pulse spiked.

He looked anxious. Determined. Like someone chasing something important.

And then, out of the shadows, the second man—hooded—stepped into view.

They didn't exchange words. Just a brief nod. Then Tyler followed him into the trees.

"That was the last known sighting," Seth said, voice low as he clicked off the surveillance footage on his monitor.

Marshall leaned back in his chair and picked up his phone. "Get Langston and Daines in here."

Within minutes, Dean Langston and Hugh Daines entered the office, both looking as though they'd just been woken from a comfortable slumber—shirts slightly rumpled, attitudes vaguely uninterested.

"Close the door," Marshall said.

Seth stood in the corner, arms crossed, silently watching as the two men made their way to the opposite side of the desk. Langston nodded politely toward Seth, but Daines barely looked at him.

"We've got a time-stamped visual of Griggs outside the trailhead entrance," Marshall said, tapping the screen. "Roughly twenty minutes before he went completely off-grid. This is the last time we see him."

Langston leaned in, squinting. "That from a trail cam?"

"Yep. Pulled it from one they no longer thought was live."

Marshall turned to Seth. "Fill them in."

Seth stepped forward, keeping his voice clipped and factual as he laid out what he and Cassie had discovered so far. The tension in the room was thick as he spoke, but not from urgency. From unease.

Because as he watched Langston and Daines—two of the sheriff's lead investigators, supposedly working this case alongside Forest Service officials and his own unit—he couldn't shake the feeling that they weren't just underperforming.

They were *deliberately* underwhelming.

Langston took a note or two, asked a few surface-level questions. Daines just folded his arms and nodded, eyes darting toward the exit like he had somewhere better to be.

And Seth couldn't forget what had just happened to him.

The Internal Affairs meeting.

A surprise visit.

Accusations of misconduct—files misfiled, false entries in logbooks, failure to report a tip related to the investigation.

It had blindsided him.

The agents had walked in like lions and walked out... confused.

There was no evidence.

Nothing stuck.

They closed the review within hours, shaking their heads and wondering why they'd been called in the first place.

But Seth knew better.

It had been a distraction. A stall. A way to keep him from digging deeper.

And now, standing in the same room as Langston and Daines, watching their non-answers and disengaged expressions...

He was starting to suspect *exactly* who had placed that anonymous tip.

They'd been assigned to assist.

But more often than not, they obstructed, delayed, rerouted.

Seth's jaw clenched as Daines asked if they could "circle back to this tomorrow."

"Someone out there knows what happened to Griggs," Marshall said, looking hard at both men. "I don't want to hear about delays. I want movement."

Langston gave a tight nod.

"We'll follow up."

But Seth didn't believe them.

Not for a second.

And as they filed out of the room, he turned to Marshall.

"You need to watch them."

Marshall's face was unreadable. "I already am."

Back at Valley Vogue, Cassie laid everything out on the boutique floor—articles, maps, emails, trail images, timelines. Kathryn sat nearby, watching her pace.

"I don't know who that man is," Cassie muttered, more to herself than to Kathryn. "But Devon trusted him. And Tyler followed him."

"Maybe it's time to ask someone who knows Devon better than you do," Kathryn suggested.

Cassie froze. "You mean Natalie."

"She's still in town, isn't she?"

Cassie nodded slowly. "We had coffee two days ago. She said she had another lead but needed time to chase it down."

"Call her."

"I will. First… I need to check something."

She pulled up her laptop and navigated to Galen Valley's public land archive. She searched for "Wren Hollow." There were a few standard maintenance logs, some trail usage permits.

Then she saw it.

A scanned land easement transfer dated ten years ago.

Two hundred acres of woodland—including the area where Tyler was last seen—had once been slated for a private development project. But the project was never completed.

Cassie clicked on the PDF.

Original grantee: *Galen Valley Community Development Initiative (GVCDI).*

Funding Partner: *Green Horizons Foundation.*

Her blood ran cold.

The Green Horizons Foundation was one of the shell donors Devon had used back in Chicago.

He'd buried funds through them to cover unethical campaigns, private favors, and PR erasures.

And now they had history in Galen Valley.

Cassie called Natalie.

"I found something," she said.

"So did I," Natalie replied. "Meet me at the overlook trail. Sunset."

Cassie hung up and went to gather her notes—but paused when she saw her laptop screen flicker.

A pop-up window opened briefly—then vanished.

She frowned.

Then noticed the message on the corner of her screen:

Remote Access Request: Accepted.

Someone had been inside her computer.

She opened her recent files.

Her trail map was gone.

So was the scanned easement.

She picked up the boutique phone to call Seth—only to hear a faint *click* on the other end.

The line had been cut.

She wasn't just being watched anymore.

She was being sabotaged.

Cassie's hands shook as she grabbed her mobile phone. The screen on her laptop still flickered beside her, glitching like a heartbeat just out of rhythm. The trail map and scanned easement had vanished, along with half her desktop files, leaving behind a corrupted mess and a chilling void.

She hit Seth's contact and pressed the phone to her ear.

He answered on the second ring.

"Cass?"

"I need you to listen," she said, her voice tight. "Someone hacked into my laptop. I found a land easement filing. Then it disappeared, along with everything else. My folders, my notes… they're just *gone.* Then I tried to call you from the boutique phone but that line has been cut."

"Damn it," Seth breathed. "Okay. Stay where you are. Lock the doors. Don't touch the laptop or the boutique phone. I'm coming over right now."

"I can't stay," Cassie said. "I'm meeting Natalie at the overlook."

"What?" His voice jumped. "Cassie, no. If someone's targeting you, the last thing you should be doing is heading into the woods alone."

"I'm not alone. Natalie's probably already there—she said it was urgent."

"Then wait for me. I'll drive you."

Cassie was already slipping on her jacket, one hand pressed to her forehead. "No. If I don't show up, she might leave or think something happened. Just meet me there, okay? Don't let anyone follow you."

Seth cursed under his breath. "I don't like this, Cass."

"I don't either," she admitted, grabbing her flashlight and stuffing it into her bag. "But if Natalie found something real, I have to hear it."

There was a pause on the line, then Seth's voice, steady and sharp. "Then don't stop for anything. Go straight there, keep your phone on, and text me the moment you arrive."

"I will."

"And Cass?" His tone dropped into something deeper.

"If anything feels off, *don't be a hero.* Just get out of there and drive straight to our house."

Cassie closed her eyes for a beat.

Then whispered, "Okay."

Cassie drove to the overlook, heart pounding, windows down. The sun was dipping low, turning the pine-lined ridge gold.

Natalie was already there—leaning against her car, arms folded.

"I found a connection," Natalie said before Cassie could speak. "The second man in that photo? I couldn't ID him directly—but I found a payroll record."

Cassie waited, holding her breath.

"Name is Michael Torrez. He was Devon's private security during the nonprofit collapse. But guess what? He also worked briefly as a consultant for the Green Horizons Foundation."

Cassie cursed under her breath. "I found a land easement filing. They tried to buy up part of Galen Valley ten years ago."

Natalie shook her head. "Of course. Devon's old playbook: fake charity, funnel money, buy silence."

"He's not just cleaning up the past," Cassie said. "He's still *using* Galen Valley."

Natalie's voice dropped. "Which means if Tyler was digging into this... he wasn't just a witness. He was a threat."

Cassie looked out over the trees below.

A storm was coming.

Again.

And this time, it wouldn't stop at whispers or graffiti.

This time, someone was going to get hurt—unless they stopped it first.

19

Seth's truck rumbled into the pull off just as Natalie's taillights disappeared around a curve. Cassie was buckling into her car when he pulled in behind her.

She rolled down the window.

"You just missed her," she said breathlessly. "She gave me good information."

"I don't like that you're out here alone," he muttered, climbing out of the truck.

"Same," she replied. "But Natalie's jumpy. Said she couldn't stay long."

He nodded toward her steering wheel. "Follow me back to the house. We'll go through it there."

Cassie hesitated only for a second, then nodded. "Okay. Let's go."

Fifteen minutes later, they pulled into Seth's long gravel driveway. But before either of them could park fully, Cassie spotted the cruiser idling near the edge of the yard.

A sheriff's department vehicle.

Seth narrowed his eyes.

"That's Baxter."

Cassie shut off her engine and leaned out her window. "Everything okay?"

Baxter Ross stepped out of the car, the twelve-pack long gone, replaced with a furrowed brow and unease in his stance.

"Hey," he said. "Sorry to drop in. I need a word."

Seth nodded. "Come in."

Inside the house, Cassie collapsed onto the living room couch, exhaustion pressing heavy against her bones. Her ears were ringing from everything that had unfolded so far.

But her focus snapped back when she heard Baxter's low voice carrying in from the kitchen.

"I've been watching Langston and Daines," Baxter said, his tone uneasy. "And I gotta be honest, Seth—I don't think they're trying to solve Griggs' case. I think they're trying to *delay it.*"

Cassie froze, leaning slightly to the side so she could hear better without being obvious.

"You're sure?" Seth asked, quiet but sharp.

"No," Baxter admitted. "That's the problem. It's all gut right now. But I've seen them 'misplace' files. Postpone field calls. There was a tip that came in last week that they didn't log for over forty-eight hours."

Seth was silent for a long beat.

"Why haven't you brought this to Marshall?"

Cassie heard Baxter sigh.

"Because Marshall's hands-off these days," he said. "He's checked out. Won't admit it, but he's distracted. And if I'm wrong, I don't want to blow a hole in the department from the inside. But if I'm right..."

Seth swore under his breath. "When we met in his office, he told me he'd be keeping an eye on those two."

Baxter scoffed. "No, Seth. He's not watching them at all. They've got *free rein* in that department. I think they know it. They're too comfortable."

Another pause. Cassie strained to hear Seth's response.

"Do you have any advice?" Baxter asked. "Something I can do to push this—without setting off alarms?"

Cassie sat up straighter.

This was it. The thread.

And someone needed to start pulling.

It started with whispers.

Then it turned into phone calls, council meeting "agenda add-ons," and passive-aggressive posts in the local Facebook group.

By the time Monday rolled around, Valley Vogue was mentioned—by name—in a petition circulating through the downtown business corridor.

The language was vague, careful.

"We, the undersigned, respectfully request that businesses engaged in on-going media controversies reconsider their roles in community-facing commerce until trust can be reestablished."

But the intent was clear.

They wanted Cassie gone.

Kathryn stood with the printout crumpled in her fist, rage flashing in her eyes.

"This is political theater," she said, pacing the boutique. "They're trying to make it sound like some neighborhood concern, but it's just about fear. And image."

"They're afraid I'll bring more attention," Cassie said quietly.

"No," Kathryn snapped. "They're afraid *they'll* be exposed."

Cassie looked at the customer appointment list for the week—half canceled. A few had left curt voicemails. One woman, a long-time client, returned an order with a sticky note that simply said: *"Disappointed."*

Cassie didn't cry.

She was beyond tears now.

She felt steel settling into her chest.

"I'm not leaving," she said.

Kathryn stopped pacing. "Good."

Kathryn walked to the checkout counter, her heels clicking sharply against the boutique floor. She pulled her phone from her purse and tapped in a number Cassie recognized by heart.

Marshall.

Cassie watched her, still seated, fingers curled tight around her mug of tea.

Kathryn held the phone to her ear. "Hey. You got a minute?"

She didn't put it on speaker at first. But a few beats into the call, her hand dropped, and the speaker came on with a quiet click—likely unintentional, maybe even instinctive. Cassie leaned back slightly, listening but not wanting to.

"Something came in today," Kathryn said, voice taut. "A printout of a petition going around town. A disgusting smear piece targeting Cassie. You know the kind. I was hoping you could look into it—see who got this started."

On the other end, Marshall exhaled.

"That's not really my lane anymore, Kathryn. Something like that falls under the mayor's office. Administrative level."

There was a long pause. Then, his voice again:

"And honestly, since it's about my wife's business and previous employee, I'd have to step back from it anyway. Conflict of interest."

Cassie could see Kathryn go rigid.

"Oh," Kathryn said, flat. "I see."

"I'm just saying, it's not personal."

"No?" Kathryn asked. "Because it *feels* personal when your town's tearing itself apart and you keep excusing yourself from the table."

Marshall sighed. "Look, I've been working nonstop. I'm heading up to the cabin later. I need some space to breathe with all this going on."

Kathryn's voice sharpened. "And *I* don't need space to breathe?"

There was silence.

"Sure, honey," Marshall replied, voice carefully neutral. "That's why *I'm* going to the cabin. You can breathe at the house."

The line clicked.

Disconnected.

Cassie stared at the phone, stunned.

Kathryn, without a word, tapped the screen to power it off, then calmly placed it back in her purse.

Her posture was perfect. Her expression unreadable.

Cassie didn't know what to say. "I—I didn't mean to overhear…"

Kathryn smiled, tight but composed. "Oh, I know. It was on me."

She stood straighter, brushing imaginary lint from her sleeve.

"Well," she said, voice smooth, "I think that's enough excitement for one afternoon."

She moved toward the door, heels even and steady.

"I'll see you in the morning, Cass."

Then she was gone.

Leaving behind silence, and the quiet hum of a woman too well-practiced at swallowing disappointment.

At the Sheriff's station, Baxter stood in a tense staff meeting as Marshall was giving them a new directive that he said came from the mayor's office: all personnel were to remain "uninvolved" in any on-going investigations related to the Griggs case unless assigned to it.

It was a thinly veiled gag order and Baxter felt targeted. Someone probably saw his patrol car at Seth's house.

"They think I'm a liability," Baxter muttered to Seth later on the phone. "They think if I speak up, I'll take the department down with me."

Seth asked, "You gonna let them do that?"

Baxter's jaw tightened. "Not a chance."

Cassie received the message that evening, slipped beneath her windshield wipers while she shopped at the corner grocery.

It wasn't typed or folded.

Just one line scrawled in black ink on torn paper.

You were never welcome here.

She stood in the lot, the paper fluttering slightly in her hand, as the sun dipped behind the trees.

That same flicker of fear sparked in her belly—but it didn't grow. Not this time.

She crumpled the note and tossed it in the bin.

Let them watch.

Let them sneer.

She wasn't going anywhere.

Natalie called an hour later with an update.

"I found him," she said. "Michael Torrez. He's off-grid but not invisible. He's in Washington now—working under a new name, but definitely the same guy."

Cassie sat on the balcony, notebook in her lap. "Is he still working for Devon?"

"No. But he's still connected. One of Devon's shell orgs funneled money to a 'security consultancy' in his name just three months ago."

Cassie exhaled. "We need to find out what he knows."

"I'm working on it," Natalie said. "But you've got to be careful. Someone's already messing with your computer, your phone... It's not just surveillance anymore. They're trying to *shut you down.*"

Cassie looked up at the darkened windows of the building across the street.

A curtain twitched.

"Let them try," she said.

The next day, the boutique was quieter than usual. Kathryn had gone to speak at a last-minute council session. Cassie sat at the counter, working through a draft for her next article when the door opened.

She looked up.

And froze.

Margaret Holloway stood in the doorway, not with her usual warmth—but with a strange distance in her eyes.

"Margaret," Cassie said slowly. "Is everything okay?"

Margaret stepped forward and set a small, sealed envelope on the counter.

"What's this?"

"Proof," Margaret said. "Of what you're up against."

Cassie opened it—and felt the ground shift beneath her.

Inside were copies of emails.

Forwarded from Margaret's inbox.

Sent from a local account, under a pseudonym—Galen_Guardian@outlook.com.

They were leaked documents. Selectively edited. Twisted. Out of context. But powerful enough to smear Cassie's public story and cast doubt on her motives.

"I don't understand," Cassie whispered. "Who sent these to you?"

Margaret's face hardened.

"Kathryn."

20

Cassie stood behind the boutique counter, one trembling hand on the envelope, the other braced on the edge of the polished wood as Margaret's words rang like a bell in her head.

"Kathryn sent them."

It didn't make sense.

Kathryn Bowen had defended her. Stood beside her. Risked her reputation for her.

And now... this?

Cassie looked up, voice sharp. "You're sure?"

"I checked the email's metadata," Margaret said quietly. "It came from an IP address linked to the boutique's account—under a name only someone close would have known."

Cassie's throat tightened. "So Kathryn's been leaking things... to *whom?*"

Margaret met her eyes. "A journalist. One who's been circling since the beginning."

Cassie's chest sank.

She knew exactly who that was.

Twenty minutes later, Cassie stood in the doorway of Kathryn's sunlit office at the back of the boutique. Her hands were cold. Her pulse thundered.

Kathryn sat at her desk, typing.

"Can we talk?" Cassie asked.

Kathryn turned, her smile faltering. "Of course."

Cassie stepped inside and closed the door behind her. "Why did you send emails about me to the press?"

Kathryn blinked. "What?"

Margaret's envelope was clenched in Cassie's hand. She tossed it onto the desk. "These."

Kathryn picked them up, eyes scanning quickly. Her brow furrowed.

"I didn't send these."

Cassie's voice was sharp. "Then how did they come from the boutique's system?"

Kathryn shook her head. "This isn't my account. It's the *store* account."

Cassie narrowed her eyes. "Who else has access?"

Silence.

Then Kathryn's eyes widened. "Hannah."

Cassie frowned. "Your niece?"

"She was helping with the newsletter and website," Kathryn said, standing. "She's been working part-time for months—doing admin tasks, social media, responding to public inquiries. I gave her login access so she could work on it remote."

Cassie's stomach dropped. "Do you trust her?"

"I thought I did," Kathryn said. "But she has been distant lately. Used to call me in the evenings and we would have lovely conversations. Now that I think about it, she only calls a few times a month and has been asking weird questions about Devon. About the store's funding. I thought she was just curious."

Margaret had been right.

Someone *was* working from within.

But it wasn't Kathryn.

It was Hannah.

Meanwhile, Seth stepped into the coffee shop where Marshall Bowen was seated with a man in a tailored gray blazer and expensive-looking watch.

The reporter.

Seth knew him instantly—Jared Blanton. He'd run the first leaked article about Cassie. Now he was back in town, ordering oat milk lattes and sniffing around for his next exclusive.

Seth approached the table with a forced smile.

"Blanton," he said. "Funny, I don't remember sending you an invitation."

Jared looked up, all slick charm. "Just here following a story, Ranger Dixon."

"Well, that story's closed."

"Is it?" Jared asked, flipping through a leather notebook. "Because I have new correspondence from an anonymous source close to Mrs. Dixon. And a few recent photos that contradict her published statements."

Seth's jaw tensed. "You're targeting a woman who's survived more than most, and a small-town sheriff's department. That doesn't make you brave. It makes you pathetic."

Blanton didn't flinch.

"I go where the truth is," he said.

Seth leaned in. "Then maybe look in the mirror."

Blanton got up, tucked his notebook under his arm and walked out.

Marshall's jaw tightened, but he didn't flinch under Seth's glare.

"You want to say something, say it," the sheriff said evenly.

Seth stepped closer, his voice low but firm. "You're sitting in plain sight with a reporter during an *open investigation*, discussing *God knows what*, while your department's lead investigators—Langston and Daines—are dragging their boots through mud, losing time and missing leads. And don't pretend you don't see it."

Marshall crossed his arms. "You're out of line, Dixon."

"No," Seth shot back. "I'm out of *patience*. You and I both know Langston and Daines have been more obstruction than help. And you've let them run unchecked."

"They're experienced men," Marshall replied, chin lifting. "They're following procedure."

"Whose procedure?" Seth snapped. "Yours? Theirs? Or the one written in invisible ink by whoever's been pulling the strings in this town since long before I put my badge on?"

Marshall's eyes darkened. "Be careful, son."

"Why?" Seth said. "Because I'm questioning authority? Or because I'm not afraid of the answer? I'm federal law enforcement. If I don't question local incompetence, who will?"

Marshall shook his head, the tension in his shoulders visible now. "You think I don't want answers too? That I don't lose sleep over Tyler Griggs?"

"Then *show it*," Seth said. "Start by holding your men accountable. And stop playing diplomat with the press while a man is still missing."

Marshall narrowed his eyes. "I didn't *give* him anything, Seth. He asked questions. I gave polite non-answers."

"You *shouldn't have been talking to him at all.*"

"I can handle a journalist," Marshall said sharply.

"No, Marshall. You *can't*, if you're compromising an active investigation in the process. You taught me that."

There was a beat of silence between them. The kind that comes between friends who have just realized they may no longer be on the same side of the line.

Seth exhaled, stepped back, and straightened his jacket.

"If you won't put your foot down, I will," he said. "Langston and Daines don't belong on this case. And if I find out they've buried even *one* more lead, I won't go through you next time. I'll go around."

Marshall didn't stop him as he walked away.

Didn't call after him.

Didn't say anything at all.

Cassie and Kathryn drove to Hannah's apartment after locking up the boutique early.

The building was quiet, shaded under thick cedar trees. Hannah's car was parked in the lot.

Cassie's hands were balled into fists as they knocked on the door.

No answer.

Kathryn pounded harder. "Hannah!"

Still nothing.

Then Cassie noticed the side window slightly open. She stepped to the edge of the porch and peered in.

Hannah's laptop was open on the kitchen counter, the glow of a video still visible on the screen. Cassie could hear a voice, she leaned in closer to listen.

"Preparing to expose a corrupt small-town narrative: the truth behind Galen Valley."

The voice in the video wasn't Hannah's.

It was Jared Blanton's.

Cassie's heart pounded. "She's feeding him *everything*."

Later that night, Cassie and Kathryn sat in the back office of the boutique, the air tense and quiet.

"I should have seen it," Kathryn said, staring into her mug of tea. "I thought she just wanted to learn."

"You trusted her," Cassie said softly. "We both did."

Kathryn looked up. "What now?"

Cassie turned her laptop around and clicked open a file.

"I write again. I don't let them control the story."

She opened a blank document.

Title:

"The Enemy Within: How Betrayal Looks a Lot Like Family"

She began typing.
Her voice, steady now.
Certain.

21

Cassie hit *publish* at 6:17 a.m.

The sky outside the boutique was still dark, the street empty except for the occasional flicker of a porch light or the shuffle of an early dog-walker.

Her hands shook slightly as she watched the article go live.

The Enemy Within: How Betrayal Looks a Lot Like Family

By Cassie Dixon

The piece was raw. More confessional than strategic. And that was intentional.

She didn't name Hannah. She didn't need to.

The story wasn't about the betrayal itself—it was about the *culture* that allowed it. About the way Galen Valley turned whispers into weapons. About what it cost to trust the wrong people. And why she wasn't going to stop now.

She closed the laptop slowly and reached for her mug. Kathryn walked in moments later, phone already buzzing.

"Brace yourself," she said. "It's spreading."

By mid-morning, the town had split cleanly down the center.

Half of Galen Valley was praising the honesty of Cassie's article, reposting it, sharing their own stories of betrayal and silence. A local teacher commented that she'd never felt more seen.

The other half accused her of stirring drama, attention-seeking, and playing victim yet again. Hannah's name wasn't in the article, but people connected the dots quickly.

Some residents called for Kathryn to be removed from the town council advisory board for "harboring instability."

Kathryn calmly ignored them.

But tension hung over every storefront, coffee shop, and sidewalk like a thundercloud.

Later that day, Cassie ducked into *Everbrew Café* to pick up a to-go order.

As she waited, a young woman approached—barely twenty, Cassie guessed, with a quiet nervousness about her.

"Mrs. Dixon?"

Cassie looked up. "Yes?"

"I just wanted to say… I read your article," the girl said. "My mom works at city hall. She said people are panicking, but I think that's a good thing. You're making them uncomfortable. That means you're close to something."

Cassie smiled, caught off guard by the insight.

"Thank you," she said.

The girl nodded. "They can't silence you now. So they'll try to bury you under noise."

Then she left.

Cassie stood there, the words echoing in her chest.

"They'll try to bury you under noise."

That evening, Seth sat in the ranger station's breakroom with an untouched soda in front of him when *she* walked in.

Leah Bennett.

One of the sheriff department's dispatchers, long-time friend, former classmate. She'd always been kind to Seth and Cassie. Always neutral. Quiet. Smart.

Tonight, she didn't look calm.

She looked… scared.

"I need to talk to you," she said, closing the door behind her.

Seth straightened. "What's wrong?"

Leah sat across from him, twisting a hair tie in her fingers.

"I've been monitoring calls from the tip line," she said. "The anonymous ones about the Griggs case."

"You think they're bogus?"

She nodded. "Most are. But there was one that got flagged—buried in the logs. It was marked as 'incomplete,' so it never hit anyone's desk, especially yours."

Seth frowned. "What did it say?"

Leah pulled a paper from her purse and unfolded it. "It was short. Just six words."

She slid it across the table.

"Don't dig up what's buried here."

Seth stared at it.

"There's more," Leah added. "The call originated from a private line… routed through a *local tower.* Not an outsider."

"You're saying someone *in* Galen Valley is trying to keep us from finding out what really happened to Griggs?"

Leah nodded. "And they have access to our system."

Seth stood, heart pounding.

Cassie had been right.

This wasn't just about a missing and presumed dead hiker or Devon Blake.

This was about *Galen Valley.*

Cassie had just set her phone on the nightstand when it buzzed.

Seth.

She answered immediately. "Hey."

"Hey," he said, his voice low, a bit rough around the edges. "Had a run-in with Marshall at the coffee shop today when I saw him talking with Blanton."

Cassie sat up straighter. "What happened?"

"I confronted him," Seth said bluntly. "Told him Langston and Daines are holding this case hostage and that if he won't do something about it, I will. He defended them—just like I figured he would."

Cassie exhaled through her nose. "And he didn't deny talking to the press?"

"Nope. Claimed he gave polite non-answers."

She frowned. "Even *polite* answers give the wrong people fuel right now."

"Exactly."

There was a pause, then Seth continued, his tone shifting. "Also… Leah showed up."

Cassie blinked. "What?"

"She came to see me. Out of nowhere. Said she wanted to talk about what happened with the tip line, and how the information is not getting to my desk."

Cassie's heart rate ticked up. "You think she was fishing for something?"

"Definitely. She dropped just enough to make it sound like she's helping, but everything about it felt off. Like a distraction. Her showing up after the confrontation with Marshall can't just be coincidental, he sent her."

Cassie bit her lip. "That's strange. I had an odd moment today too. A girl stopped me at Everbrew. Said her mom works for the city and that people are panicking because I am getting too close.'"

There was silence on the other end of the line. Then Seth said, "Damn."

"Yeah," Cassie said softly. "They're circling, Seth. Whoever's behind this—they're tightening the noose. Random people don't come talk to me for no reason."

"Then it's time we pull tighter in return," he said. "I want to get together with Baxter in the next day or two. At the house. Quietly."

Cassie nodded, even though he couldn't see it. "Yeah. That makes sense. I'll be there."

"I'll reach out to him and let you know what time."

"Okay," she said. "Be safe."

"You too," he replied.

She hung up and stared at the phone in her hand for a long moment.

Then she got up, crossed to the glass door of her tiny balcony, and stepped out into the night air.

The streets below were still and empty. But Cassie knew better.

The town wasn't sleeping.

It was *watching*.

And somewhere in the dark—

Everything was shifting.

Truth was coming to the surface.

Someone didn't want her to know what she was about to find out.

22

The sun was just rising when Cassie and Seth reached the trail-head at Wren Hollow.

They stood in silence, listening to the forest breathe. This time, Cassie had traded her usual boots for a pair of sturdy hiking ones, borrowed from Kathryn. Her backpack held a notebook, extra batteries, a portable GPS, and the photo—the one with Devon and the hooded man.

"You sure you're up for this?" Seth asked, adjusting his pack.

Cassie didn't hesitate. "Someone wanted us to *not* come here. That's exactly why we should."

They hiked for an hour before the trees started to thin and the path curved into the dense clearing shown in the trail cam footage. Seth walked ahead, scanning for familiar landmarks. Cassie kept her gaze low, searching for anything out of place—disturbed earth, something caught in the brush.

They found it together.

A glint of silver, half-buried beneath pine needles and damp soil, caught Seth's eye.

He crouched, brushing it off.

A phone. Cracked. Weathered. But still intact.

Tyler Griggs' phone.

Seth looked up. "We need to get this to forensics."

Cassie nodded. "We need to make a copy of whatever's on it first."

Back at the ranger station, Seth and Cassie plugged the recovered phone into an offline laptop. The device booted slowly, the screen flickering through water-damaged pixels.

But it worked.

Most of the photos and messages were gone.

Except one.

A voice memo, timestamped just two days before Tyler disappeared.

Cassie clicked play.

"If something happens to me, it's because I got too close. The man I met—he didn't want to talk. He wanted to warn me. Told me the 'valley was built on two things: beauty and blood.' Said the town had secrets that never made it to courtrooms. I think this goes deeper than Devon. I think someone local has been helping him. And I think Cassie Dixon has no idea what she's standing on."

The recording cut out.

Cassie stared at the screen, the weight of his voice pressing down on her chest.

"Beauty and blood."

Meanwhile, Natalie paced the perimeter of the boutique, phone pressed to her ear, heart racing.

She wasn't expecting to get a blocked call.

She *really* wasn't expecting to hear his voice.

"Still chasing ghosts, Nat?" Devon said, voice like velvet soaked in venom.

Her stomach turned. "What do you want?"

"Just wanted to say hello. Heard you and Cassie have been stirring things up."

"We found the footage. The payments. The trail cam. It's over."

Devon chuckled. "It's *never* over. And you're not as invisible as you think. Nice job dragging Torrez out of hiding. Brave move."

Natalie's grip tightened. "You killed Tyler."

"No," Devon said casually. "But someone local might've helped. And if I were you, I'd watch who you trust."

The line went dead.

Natalie stood in the alley behind Valley Vogue, her hand shaking.

Cassie wasn't the only one being hunted.

At the same time, across town, fire trucks roared past Elliot's old rental—now empty—heading toward the industrial edge of Galen Valley.

A warehouse near the trailhead had gone up in flames.

The structure was mostly abandoned, used occasionally for storage.

But the firemen reported something strange: inside the building, just before the fire started, someone had spray-painted four words across the back wall in dripping red paint.

"STOP DIGGING OR BURN"

Marshall stood outside the smoke and flashing lights, arms folded, jaw set.

He'd seen a lot in his years in Galen Valley.

But something about this...

It didn't feel like a warning.

It felt like a declaration.

The smoke had long since cleared from the burned-out warehouse, but the smell still lingered faintly in the air.

Cassie sat on the edge of the couch in Kathryn's upstairs apartment, wrapped in a throw blanket, her tea now cold on the coffee table. Natalie paced the small living room behind her, arms folded tightly.

"They meant for someone to be inside that warehouse," Natalie said, voice sharp with fear. "That timing? That fire? It wasn't just a warning."

"I know," Cassie said softly, her gaze fixed on the floor. "But thankfully no one was hurt."

Natalie exhaled hard. "Doesn't matter. They're getting bold. Whoever they are."

She stopped pacing and turned toward Cassie.

"I haven't even told you the worst of it."

Cassie finally looked up.

Natalie sat down across from her, lowering her voice. "I got a call. A blocked number. I answered because it rang three times in a row."

Cassie leaned in. "And?"

"Devon."

Cassie froze.

Natalie nodded. "Sounded calm. Too calm. Said he'd seen the fire. Said things were 'shifting' in Galen Valley. That soon, the 'real founders' would take their place again."

Cassie felt a chill crawl across her skin.

"Did he threaten you?"

"No," Natalie said. "Not directly. But he said I should stop chasing ghosts. That not all stories need an ending."

Cassie stood, wrapping the blanket tighter around her.

"So he's watching. From where, we don't know."

"I've already reported it to the feds," Natalie said. "They're looking into it. But I doubt they'll find him if he doesn't want to be found."

Cassie walked toward the window, the town lights flickering against the glass.

"They're trying to scare us into silence," she said. "Fires. Phone calls. Rumors. Surveillance."

Natalie rose too. "They don't know us very well, do they?"

Cassie gave a faint smile. "Apparently not."

Natalie gathered her things, pulling on her coat. "I'm heading back to the hotel. But if you need anything—"

Cassie turned and hugged her. "Thank you. For everything."

When Natalie left, the apartment felt too quiet.

Cassie sat back down by the window, pulled her knees to her chest, and stared out at the town that never seemed to stop testing her.

That night, Cassie stared out the window of the boutique's apartment, her laptop open beside her, a single sentence flashing on the screen of her unfinished article.

"I thought I was running from the past—but it turns out, the past was always walking one step behind me."

She closed the lid slowly.

The fire. The phone. The voice memo. Devon's shadow creeping back in.

There was no running anymore.

There was only the choice to stand and fight.

23

The warehouse fire made the local paper's front page by morning, but the article was thin on facts.

No suspects.

No witnesses.

No cause determined.

Cassie knew better.

Someone had torched it on purpose. The message on the wall made that clear—and if it hadn't, the second message she found scrawled on the back windshield of her car later that morning confirmed it:

"Stay quiet or disappear."

She had looked at it for a long time before wiping it off with one clean stroke of her sleeve.

"Let them watch," she'd muttered. "But they don't get to silence me."

The sky was still that soft pre-dawn gray when Cassie pulled into Seth's driveway, gravel crunching under her tires. Morning fog clung to the trees like a breath that hadn't yet exhaled. She was early—but not the first to arrive.

Baxter's cruiser was already there.

Cassie grabbed her bag and headed up the steps. The porch light was on, welcoming in a way it hadn't felt in a long time. She paused for just a moment before knocking once and stepping inside.

The scent hit her immediately—eggs, bacon, biscuits, and that warm, buttery note of gravy bubbling on the stove.

Seth stood at the range in jeans and a long-sleeved henley, spatula in hand. Baxter leaned against the counter nursing a mug of coffee, his badge clipped to his belt but his eyes weary.

"Well look who's here," Seth said with a soft smile, nodding her toward the plates already stacked at the edge of the counter. "Grab a plate before Baxter eats it all."

Cassie smiled faintly, grateful for the comfort of routine in the chaos. "Wouldn't miss it."

She made her way to the food and loaded her plate—eggs, bacon, a flaky biscuit split open to soak up the gravy. The smells wrapped around her like an old sweater.

She moved to the fridge to grab the orange juice and coffee pot. As she reached for the cups in the top cabinet, her hand froze mid-motion.

It was muscle memory.

She knew exactly where everything was. The plates, the glasses, the filters for the coffee, the cinnamon Seth sometimes sprinkled into it when she couldn't sleep.

She turned slowly, looking over her shoulder at the kitchen—the light bouncing off the metal kettle, the dented breadbox by the toaster, the photograph still pinned to the fridge of the two of them at last year's Founders' Day picnic.

It was good.

And weird.

Like stepping back into a room preserved in time, even though everything around them had changed.

Seth noticed the hesitation. Their eyes met across the kitchen.

And just like that—there it was.

That shared look. Soft. Familiar. Loaded with every unsaid word and every scar they'd ever tried to bandage over.

Cassie blinked once, then turned back to her coffee.

She brought her mug and glass of juice to the table and sat down.

She and Seth instinctively slid into their old spots—as if nothing had changed. But everything had. Eyes locked on each other.

The first few minutes passed in silence, the kind that was less awkward and more... *anchored.* They needed a moment to just *be.* Baxter had started digging into his food, oblivious to what was happening at the table.

Cassie finally broke the gaze with Seth and dug into her plate, the food grounding her.

Then she set her fork down.

"Alright," she said, wiping her hands on a napkin. "Let's get to it."

Seth leaned forward, elbows on the table. "We've got to break this down—piece by piece. What we know, what we suspect, and what Baxter's been hearing inside the department."

Cassie nodded. "Starting with the obvious. Langston and Daines. We've all seen it—they're either covering something up, or they're being used by someone who is."

Baxter set his coffee down, his jaw tight. "I've tried to watch them, but they're cagey. They rarely talk around other deputies. Stay tight-lipped and close to each other. If they're working something behind the scenes, they're keeping it sealed."

"Have they said anything about the missing hiker?" Seth asked.

"Nothing that makes sense," Baxter said. "They go through the motions, sure. But it's bare minimum. Almost like they want to drag it out until it goes cold."

Cassie frowned. "That's a tactic. Exhaust the urgency. Let the case fade into the background."

Baxter nodded grimly. "Exactly. And you want to know the worst part?"

Cassie glanced up. "There's more?"

"They're in Marshall's office *constantly,*" Baxter said. "Closed doors. No logs, no reports getting filed from those conversations. Whatever they're talking about, it's off the books."

Seth leaned back, eyes narrowing. "I asked Marshall if he was watching them. He said he was."

Baxter snorted. "Then he's either lying or asleep at the wheel. They've got *free rein*. He's not checking anything."

Cassie exhaled sharply. "So either Marshall's complicit, or he's been sidelined in his own department."

"Or worse," Seth said darkly, "he's choosing to look the other way."

No one responded for a beat.

Then Cassie said, "We need leverage. Something real. If we're going to confront this, it can't just be instinct."

Baxter nodded. "I've got eyes and ears. I'll keep pressing. But we're going to have to be careful."

Seth tapped his fingers against his coffee mug, thinking. "Let's plan something. A strategy. If we can shake loose one piece of evidence—even a slip—we can start pulling the thread."

Cassie sat back in her chair and looked between the two men.

For the first time in weeks, she didn't feel like she was fighting alone.

Later that day, Cassie and Natalie met at the edge of Whispering Pines Trail, a lesser-known path that wound behind Wren Hollow and into county-owned land. They weren't here to hike.

They were following a breadcrumb.

Natalie had gotten a tip through an old digital activist group—a burner phone ping tied to Michael Torrez had recently resurfaced just outside a ranger-monitored zone. Whoever he was now, he wasn't hiding far.

They hiked in silence until they reached the overlook. Natalie scanned the horizon, eyes sharp.

"He's here," she said. "He's watching. Always was."

Cassie looked down the valley.

"If he's still working for Devon, we'll never see him coming."

"Then we stop playing defense," Natalie said. "We take the story public. We name names. Every name."

Cassie hesitated. "That means implicating people in Galen Valley. People who *aren't* ready to be exposed."

Natalie turned toward her, eyes hard. "They were ready to protect secrets. They're fair game."

At the ranger station, Seth returned from a field patrol to find Baxter in his office with a locked evidence box on the desk.

Seth raised an eyebrow. "What's that?"

"Evidence pulled from the warehouse fire," Baxter said. "A cell phone. Unregistered. Melted beyond use, but the SIM card survived."

"Anything on it?"

Baxter hesitated. "Yeah. A deleted photo backup. It pinged off the same server that accessed Cassie's old files a few weeks ago."

Seth's jaw tightened. "So whoever torched the warehouse was also the one spying on her?"

"Looks that way."

Baxter leaned in, voice low. "I need to tell you something, Seth. Something I should've told you a week ago."

Seth's stomach flipped.

"What?"

"I found an encrypted drive hidden in an old evidence locker," Baxter said. "It was never logged. No tag. Just buried beneath false labels. When I opened it, I found audio clips, reports… internal memos."

"Memos about what?"

"About the *foundation* that tried to buy out Wren Hollow years ago. The same one Devon funneled money through."

Seth went pale. "Someone on the inside knew it was happening."

Baxter nodded grimly. "And they hid it."

Meanwhile, Cassie sat in the backroom of Valley Vogue, uploading her next article.

The title was blunt. She was done softening.

"They Tried to Burn the Evidence—Here's What We Found"

The piece laid it all out: the trail camera footage, the burner phone, the fire, the messages. She didn't accuse anyone directly, but she didn't need to.

The comments section was open.

Within an hour, it had over 200 shares—and one anonymous comment that stood out:

"Ask Detective Langston about March 3rd. The locker wasn't empty."

Cassie's blood went cold.

Langston who in her view was actively sabotaging the investigation into the disappearance of Tyler Griggs.

If *he* had something to do with suppressing evidence…

She didn't finish the thought.

She picked up her phone and dialed Seth.

"We have a problem," she said. "And it's wearing a badge."

Late that evening, Seth made a visit to the Sheriff's department and pulled Marshall aside.

"We need to look at Langston," he said quietly. "Something's off."

To Seth's surprise, Marshall didn't argue.

They opened the internal logbooks for March 3rd—cross-referencing keycard access with the evidence locker timestamps.

Langston's name was there.

At 4:43 a.m.

Hours before the SIM card had been found in the burned warehouse.

"He moved it," Marshall whispered. "He knew the building was going up in flames."

Seth nodded, fury rising. "And he let us chase shadows while he cleaned up the real trail."

Marshall sat back in his chair, looking suddenly older than Seth had ever seen him.

"This goes deep," the sheriff said. "And it started long before Cassie ever showed up."

Across town, Natalie sat in her car with her laptop open.

A new email had arrived in her encrypted inbox.

No subject line.

Just a name.

Michael Torrez

And a location.

Hollow Ridge Campground – Wednesday. Come alone.

Natalie exhaled shakily and texted Cassie one word:

Bait?

Cassie's reply came fast.

Trap.

24

"Marshall," Seth's voice was steady, quiet. "What do you mean this started long before Cassie ever showed up."

Marshall sighed and just looked at him. "It did."

"Well, then tell me what you know."

Marshall hesitated.

"No more vague warnings, Marshall. No more dodging. What do you *know* that you're not telling me?"

The air between them thickened with the weight of years—mentorship, loyalty, tension, silence.

Marshall looked over his shoulder out the window, then leaned towards the desk and motioned for Seth to lean closer in on his side.

"I was a deputy when the last land scandal broke wide open. You would've been in middle school. Most people barely remember it now—hell, most of the old-timers won't talk about it."

Seth said nothing, just waited.

"There was a man," Marshall continued. "Elijah Griggs. Tyler's grandfather. He worked the forestry contract before it was restructured into the federal program we have now. Good man. Quiet. Kept to himself. But one day, he came into my office shaking like a leaf. Said he'd found old land grant files in a hollow behind Sage Hill. Records that didn't match county archives. Handwritten deeds. Transfer notes. Names that didn't show up in public records."

Seth furrowed his brow. "Like Hollinger?"

Marshall nodded slowly. "That name was one of them."

"And what happened?"

"I took it to the sheriff at the time—Dawson Carrow. He told me to burn it. Said the town had survived worse and didn't need ghosts rising up. I didn't burn it." Marshall paused, jaw tightening. "But someone else did. Griggs' trailer burned down two nights later. He survived. Barely. Moved his family out of town within a week."

Seth felt something cold settle in his chest. "Tyler came back years later. No one knew who he really was until he vanished."

"Exactly," Marshall said. "And when that boy went missing, all I could think was: it's happening again. Somebody knows that kid's family had a history here. Knew his name. Knew what his grandfather found."

"And Langston and Daines?" Seth asked.

Marshall's eyes narrowed. "I didn't assign them to this case. They were *placed.* Showed up with orders from higher up. Said they were running point because of jurisdiction overlap. I didn't argue. Maybe I should've."

"You let them take it over."

Marshall flinched. "I thought they'd just do what needed doing. That they'd clear it or bury it—either way, it'd be off our books. But I didn't think they'd sabotage the damn thing."

Seth took a step closer, eyes sharp. "So why haven't you stopped them?"

Marshall looked away.

"I've been part of this machine for a long time, Seth. Longer than I like to admit. Some days, it's hard to tell where loyalty ends and guilt begins."

"That's not good enough," Seth snapped.

"I know."

"I need you to help me fix this."

Marshall shook his head. "You don't need me anymore. You've already started tearing it down. Me? I'm already too deep in the foundation."

Seth stared at him.

Disgusted.

Disappointed.

Heartbroken.

Then he turned and walked away.

Marshall didn't stop him.

Didn't follow.

Didn't say another word.

The Hollow Ridge Campground was nearly deserted.

Midweek. Off-season. Cold enough that the only sounds were wind through skeletal trees and the occasional creak of an aging picnic bench.

Natalie parked her car in the gravel lot and left her phone in the glove compartment, as instructed. She slipped her old press badge into her pocket—not because she expected it to protect her, but because it gave her hands something to clutch if things went sideways.

And they *would*.

They always did when Devon Blake's name was involved.

Cassie paced the length of the boutique's back room, phone pressed to her ear. "She's there now."

Seth's voice came through the other end, sharp. "Alone?"

"She insisted. Said she could handle it."

"Where?"

"Hollow Ridge Campground."

"I'll meet you," Seth said. "We'll stay off-site. Just in case it's a trap."

Cassie grabbed her coat and keys. "I have a bad feeling."

"You should," Seth muttered. "Because if this is who we think it is, Natalie just walked into a predator's den."

Natalie spotted the man leaning against a tree near the fire ring—gray hoodie, boots coated in trail dust, head down.

Michael Torrez.

He hadn't aged much.

Still had that tight, coiled stance of someone who never stopped scanning the edges.

"You came," he said without looking up.

"I don't scare easy," Natalie replied, stopping a safe ten feet away.

"Could've fooled me. You ran fast enough when everything went down."

Natalie crossed her arms. "So did you. Or are you still working for Devon?"

He looked at her now. "That's what you came to ask?"

"I came for the truth."

Torrez gave a low laugh. "That's the problem with truth. People say they want it, but the second you hand it to them, they drop it like a grenade."

Natalie didn't flinch. "Did you meet with Tyler Griggs?"

"Briefly."

"Did you lead him into the woods that day?"

"I tried to warn him off," Torrez said. "Told him to walk away. Told him he didn't know who he was chasing."

"Did you kill him?"

His jaw tightened. "No. But I saw who did."

Natalie's pulse spiked. "Who?"

Torrez stepped forward. "The man who's been in this town longer than you've been alive. The one wearing a badge while the rest of you sleep."

Natalie took a step back. "You mean Sheriff Marshall Bowen?"

Torrez didn't answer.

But he didn't deny it.

Seth and Cassie arrived at the edge of the campground, headlights off, the engine rumbling low. They moved fast and quiet, ducking behind a thicket of trees just as Natalie raised her voice.

Cassie saw the man—tall, broad, dangerous. Not visibly armed. But she didn't trust the tension in his shoulders or the way his hand hovered near his pocket.

"She's too close," Cassie whispered.

Seth already had his hand on his holster.

They stepped out together.

"Natalie!" Cassie shouted.

Torrez spun, startled—but didn't run.

Instead, he smiled.

"Well, well," he said. "The ghost herself."

"Hands where I can see them," Seth said, stepping forward, voice low and lethal.

Torrez raised his hands, slowly.

"No weapons," he said. "Not today."

Natalie turned toward Cassie, pale. "He says Marshall—"

"I heard," Cassie replied.

Seth didn't lower his weapon.

"You're gonna need to come with us," he told Torrez. "We're going to have a long conversation back at the ranger station."

But Torrez never made it there.

As they walked him to the car, a black SUV crested the hill behind them—no lights, no plates.

The doors opened.

Cassie didn't see who stepped out.

But Torrez did.

His face changed instantly—eyes narrowing, jaw locking. Then, with a sudden twist, he shoved Seth sideways and bolted into the woods.

"Torrez!" Seth yelled, giving chase.

Cassie grabbed Natalie and ducked behind the car as a single *crack* echoed through the clearing.

Gunfire.

Not at them.

At Torrez.

Another shot.

Then silence.

Seth returned moments later, pale and furious. "He's gone."

Cassie swallowed. "Dead?"

"Didn't see him fall. But whoever's out there… they don't want him talking."

Natalie looked at them both.

"He told me something else."

"What?" Cassie asked.

"He said Devon's not the top of the chain."

"Then who is?"

Natalie met her eyes.

"He said *Galen Valley* is."

25

They called an emergency town hall meeting.

By noon, every pew in the Galen Valley Community Center was filled. Residents buzzed with suspicion, tension, and just enough outrage to tip the room into chaos with a single match.

Cassie sat near the back, flanked by Kathryn on one side and Natalie on the other, trying not to flinch as someone behind her whispered her name like it was poison.

"She's the reason for all of this…"

"If she'd never come here…"

Seth stood near the front with Marshall, arms crossed, a storm in his eyes. Neither of them had slept. After the Hollow Ridge ambush, Torrez had disappeared like smoke. Whether he was alive or dead, they couldn't confirm. The SUV was gone. The woods silent.

But they knew what they'd seen.

And they knew someone in that very room wanted them to forget it.

Mayor Denise Carrow took the stage first. She was polished, controlled, but her eyes betrayed her nerves.

"We've heard the concerns," she began. "And in light of recent events—including the warehouse fire, the unsanctioned press coverage, and the continued speculation around the Tyler Griggs investigation—we felt it necessary to bring this community together."

She didn't mention Cassie by name.

But the way the room turned to glare said enough.

Someone from the business council stood.

"We'd like to request a vote to suspend all town contracts and official collaborations with any residents currently under public scrutiny—particularly those with ties to ongoing investigations."

A few people clapped.

Cassie's heart thudded in her chest.

Kathryn stood up fast, voice clear and cutting. "That's not a motion. That's a threat disguised as a policy."

Gasps. Murmurs.

"Valley Vogue is a privately owned business," she said, turning to the crowd. "And if you want to punish women for telling the truth, you'd better be ready to explain what *you're* hiding."

Mayor Carrow held up her hand. "Enough."

Then someone else stood.

Someone Cassie hadn't seen in months.

Leah Bennett.

The dispatcher.

Seth stiffened.

"I have something to say," Leah said.

She walked toward the front, face pale, voice shaking—but resolute.

"I was asked to erase a call," she said. "Back in March. A tip that came through the emergency line. It warned about what happened to Tyler Griggs. It mentioned a location, a name. It was flagged as 'noise' and deleted before anyone could trace it."

The room buzzed louder.

Seth stepped forward. "Who gave you that order?"

Leah looked directly at Sheriff Marshall Bowen.

Gasps exploded like fireworks. Kathryn jumped up again and started toward the front but Cassie and Natalie held her back. She turned to look at Cassie with tears in her eyes and allowed them to sit her back down.

Marshall stood, mouth opening—but Seth was already moving.

"You're done," Seth said.

He motioned for two of his deputy rangers to escort Marshall out. The man didn't resist, his expression was blank as he passed Cassie. She could feel Kathryn shaking beside her.

"This meeting is over," Cassie muttered to Kathryn, "let's get you out of here."

She didn't even blink or say a word but allowed Cassie and Natalie to lead her out of the building.

Outside, reporters swarmed the parking lot, jostling for sound bites.

"Cassie! Did you know about the deleted call?"

"Kathryn! Did you know your husband was sabotaging the investigation?"

"Cassie! Are you planning to leave Galen Valley again?"

"Kathryn! What's your husband's connection to Tyler Griggs?"

Cassie and Natalie pushed through flanking Kathryn on both sides, ignoring the noise.

They didn't owe them answers.

But inside, Cassie's mind reeled.

Marshall wasn't the ringleader.

He was the gatekeeper.

And someone else—someone higher, smarter, more protected—was still pulling the strings.

That evening, Elliot's name lit up on her phone.

Elliot Rhodes

1 Missed Call

1 Voicemail

Cassie sat on the balcony and listened.

"Hey... I saw the town hall stuff online. It's getting ugly. Just say the word, Cass, and I'll come back. We'll drive until the map runs out. But if you're staying... then fight. And I'll fight with you. Even from here."

Cassie closed her eyes.

Fighting felt impossible.

But so did running now.

The steel door clanked shut behind Seth as he walked away from the holding cell. Marshall Bowen sat on the bench inside, quiet, staring at the floor, his badge resting beside him like it weighed more now than it ever had before.

Seth locked the door and slid the key into his pocket.

He had barely made it three steps toward the front of the station when the glass doors burst open.

Langston and Daines.

Their boots hit the floor like gunshots.

"We want him out," Langston barked.

Seth didn't flinch. "Marshall stays where he is. He's being held until the FBI arrive."

Langston's jaw clenched. "You don't have that authority. You have *no* jurisdiction to hold a sitting sheriff."

"Then go get a release from a federal judge," Seth replied evenly. "Come back with an order and I'll let him out. Until then? He stays."

Daines cursed under his breath. "You know damn well we won't get that in time."

"Not if you stand here wasting more breath on me," Seth countered. "Tick tock, gentlemen. The Bureau's on the road and last I checked, I don't answer to you. So unless you plan to stand there like a pair of wind-up toys, I suggest you leave."

Langston stepped forward, fists clenched at his sides.

He reared back like he meant to swing.

Seth took a single step closer, eyes burning with the kind of fire only truth and fury can fuel.

"Oh *please*, Langston," he said, voice like a blade. "I *beg* you. Take a swing at me. It'll be the *last thing* you do."

He gestured toward the row of cells.

"I've got another empty one right next to Marshall's. Go ahead. Give me a reason to lock you up too."

Daines grabbed Langston's shoulder just in time, yanking him back.

Langston's face was crimson with rage, his fists trembling. But he didn't move again.

"Let's go," Daines muttered. "Not here. Not now."

They turned and stormed out, boots thundering against the linoleum, the door slamming behind them.

Moments later, the roar of their cruiser echoed through the parking lot—followed by a spray of gravel as they peeled out, rocks pinging off the side of the ranger trucks.

"Hey!" one of the deputy rangers shouted, rising from the bench. "I'm going after them—"

Seth raised a hand. "Let it go, Foster. Not worth it. We've got bigger fish to fry."

The deputy hesitated, then nodded, retreating back to his desk.

Seth walked back toward the cells and paused outside Marshall's.

The sheriff looked up, eyes still cloudy, defeated but not quite broken.

"Go see if you can get a statement from him," Seth said to Foster. "Before he shakes the shock and lawyers up."

Foster nodded and headed toward the back.

Seth stood there for a long moment, watching the door, listening to the silence.

Everything had changed.

But at least now, *he* was finally the one steering the ship.

At the same time, Natalie pulled a single envelope from her bag. She'd been holding it for weeks, unsure what to do with it.

Inside: Devon's original project bid for the Green Horizons Foundation's Galen Valley development.

It was signed by three people.

Devon Blake.

Michael Torrez.

And...

Mayor Denise Carrow.

26

The envelope sat in the center of Kathryn's kitchen table, its edges worn from Natalie's nervous fingers. Cassie stared down at the contract, the three signatures lined up like ghosts waiting for judgment.

Devon Blake.

Michael Torrez.

And Mayor Denise Carrow.

"She lied to everyone," Natalie whispered. "About the foundation. About the development deal. She buried this right alongside everything else."

Cassie nodded slowly. "And she's still in charge."

"Which means she's still covering her tracks."

Cassie opened her laptop. "Not for long."

Seth sat in his truck outside the ranger station, watching as FBI investigators loaded boxes from the evidence room into the back of a black SUV.

He had called in the higher-ups. Marshall's arrest had exposed more than misconduct—it had unraveled a network of misfiled reports, missing timestamps, and strategic erasures going back *years*.

"We've lost the town's trust," Baxter said quietly, standing beside the truck.

"We never had it," Seth replied. "Not really. Not since Tyler went missing. Maybe not even before that."

Baxter turned to him. "You can walk away now. Turn it all over to the FBI. Nobody would blame you."

Seth looked out at the pines beyond the lot. "If I walk now, I'm no better than the ones who kept quiet."

Baxter gave a solemn nod. "Then stay. But understand—what comes next won't be clean."

Cassie and Natalie stood in Kathryn's kitchen, stacks of papers and old emails spread across the counter. They were building a timeline. Connecting names, companies, properties.

Kathryn was still asleep on the couch in the adjacent family room. She had taken some anxiety medication when they first brought her home, laid down and immediately drifted off to sleep.

Cassie paused as she spotted a name buried in the fine print of a grant application tied to the Green Horizons Foundation.

Cypress West Consulting

"I know this name," Cassie said, heart pounding.

"It's one of Devon's fronts," Natalie confirmed. "It was used to launder campaign funds. Why?"

Cassie flipped the file around and pointed to the recipient.

"Payment: $20,000 retainer fee issued to CWC—signed off by Denise Carrow, then Director of Regional Development."

Natalie blinked. "So she wasn't just part of the Galen Valley project. She *greenlit* the money trail."

Cassie stood straight. "We need to publish. Everything. Tonight."

Natalie hesitated. "You're ready to go all the way?"

Cassie nodded. "Let them try to bury me again. This time, I'm dragging the whole valley with me."

Meanwhile, Denise Carrow sat in her office at Town Hall, jaw tight as she read the preliminary story teaser already circulating online.

"Coming Tonight: Galen Valley's Forgotten Deal—A Mayor's Signature, a Missing Hiker, and a Decade of Secrets"

Her assistant peeked in. "You've got two news outlets holding for comment."

Denise didn't answer.

Instead, she opened her desk drawer, pulled out a burner phone, and typed one message.

"Contain this."

She hit send.

Then lit the phone on fire in a glass ashtray.

As the sun dipped behind the hills, the article went live on *Medium* and syndicated through a network of journalists Cassie had quietly built since her original story. Natalie added the receipts. Cassie's voice carried the fire.

"This isn't just about me. This is about power. About privilege. About what happens when small towns get too good at hiding their sins beneath the pines."

Screenshots. Payment logs. Grant documents. Whistleblower notes. It was all there.

The backlash was instant.

The town's Facebook group exploded.

Half called for Denise Carrow's resignation. The other half screamed slander. But no one was silent.

Later that night, when Cassie arrived at the boutique after leaving Kathryn's, Seth was waiting for her. She made them both some tea in the apartment and they sat on the balcony looking over the town. The street below them was quiet—like the town was holding its breath again.

"Are you scared?" Seth asked.

Cassie looked at him, tired but steady. "Terrified."

"But not backing down."

"Never again."

Seth nodded. "Then I'm staying close. Just in case someone decides to get desperate."

Cassie smiled, but only faintly.

"I've been thinking," he said carefully. "Maybe you should come back to the house."

Cassie's head snapped around to look him in the eye.

"Why?"

"Security," Seth said plainly. "If someone's watching you—and I believe they are—then I'd rather you be where I know every door, every window, and every shadow. At least there I can keep you safe."

She studied him for a moment, then shook her head. "Seth…"

He crossed his arms. "I'm serious, Cass."

"I know," she said gently. "But I don't want to put you in danger."

"You wouldn't be."

She raised a hand to stop him. "You know that's not true. I'm the center of all this. If I come back to that house, I bring the danger with me. And on top of that…" Her voice dropped. "I'm not sure being that close to you wouldn't complicate things. For both of us."

Seth's face shifted, not with surprise—but with the weight of truth settling between them.

She continued, "You're in the middle of the investigation. The FBI already has eyes on everything. If I'm sleeping under your roof while also holding evidence tied to the missing hiker case and Devon Blake, it could look like collusion. I don't want to risk that—for your sake."

"You think I care about optics right now?"

"I think you *should*." Cassie said. "You've worked too hard to be taken seriously by federal investigators. I won't be the reason they start questioning your judgment."

Seth's jaw tightened. For a moment, she thought he might push harder.

But then he reached into his coat and pulled out a small black pistol.

Cassie blinked.

He offered it, grip first.

"It's yours," he said quietly. "Remember? I got it for you after I started pulling late shifts when we first moved to Galen Valley. You were nervous being home alone."

She stared at it, memories flickering across her face.

"It's loaded," he added. "Safety's easy to switch. You remember?"

Cassie took it with both hands and nodded. "I remember."

He gave a half-smile. "Just for added protection. I hope you won't need it."

"I hope so too," she said, voice softening. "But... thank you. For thinking of me. For bringing it."

"Always."

Cassie walked him to the back door of the boutique. They paused beneath the security light that flickered occasionally but held steady enough tonight to cast them both in a warm, amber glow.

Neither said much as she unlocked the door, then opened it for him to step outside.

He turned back to face her, his hand briefly brushing her arm.

"You call me if *anything* feels off," he said. "Even if it's just a shadow you don't like."

"I will."

She closed the door.

He stayed on the other side, listening.

He heard the deadbolt slide home.

Then the keypad beeped: *armed.*

That familiar pattern of clicks and tones was both comforting and suffocating.

She was locked in.

He was locked out.

Seth walked slowly to his car, glancing up once at the windows above the boutique.

He didn't like this—her alone, vulnerable, a target in plain sight.

But he respected her choice.

He slid into the driver's seat, started the engine, and pulled away—still gripping the wheel harder than necessary, the image of her standing in that doorway burned behind his eyes.

27

Cassie was in the apartment above the boutique, curled under a throw blanket with her laptop open and a stack of notes scattered across the coffee table. The hum of the streetlights outside was the only sound—until it wasn't.

CRASH.

The first brick shattered the front display window.

Cassie jolted upright, heart hammering in her chest.

CRASH. CRASH.

Two more bricks came flying through the glass downstairs.

The boutique alarm screamed to life, a deafening wail that pierced the quiet and sent her blood surging with adrenaline.

Cassie jumped to her feet, scrambled to the drawer near the kitchenette, and yanked it open. Her fingers wrapped around the cold grip of the pistol Seth had brought her.

She moved quickly but carefully, the weapon heavy in her hand, her bare feet flying down the stairs.

She reached the shattered front windows just in time to see a black SUV speeding away, tires screeching against the pavement. It was nearly identical to the one they had seen the day Natalie met Michael Torrez at the campground.

Cassie bolted behind the counter, grabbed the landline phone, and punched in three digits with trembling fingers.

"911, what's your emergency?"

"This is Cassie Dixon at Valley Vogue. Someone just threw bricks through the front windows—three of them. The alarm's going off and I saw a black SUV speeding away. I need officers *now*."

The dispatcher's voice was calm but urgent. "Officers are on the way. Stay inside. Do not approach the windows."

Cassie clutched the pistol tighter and waited, the sirens growing louder within minutes.

Town police and county deputies arrived in unison, lights flashing red and blue across the boutique's now-glass-strewn floor. One officer gently nudged Cassie aside to examine the bricks scattered among shards of glass and torn curtains.

"What's this?" a deputy muttered, crouching down.

Wrapped around each brick was a piece of lined paper, secured by rubber bands.

He unfurled one, then another.

Handwritten threats in thick black marker.

"Go back to where you came from, Cassie."

"You're not safe here."

Another one was addressed to Kathryn:

"This town was better before your heels hit its sidewalks."

Cassie felt her knees weaken.

Just then, the door opened behind her and two figures stepped through—Baxter and Seth.

They looked around at the damage, the crowd of officers, and the expressions of every deputy in the room.

Seth's eyes went straight to Cassie.

She turned to him, clutching the gun at her side. "It was the same SUV. I swear, Seth—it was the one from the campground."

"We're not waiting anymore," Seth said firmly, his jaw tight. "You're coming home with me. Tonight."

Cassie opened her mouth to argue but closed it again. Her shoulders sagged with exhaustion.

"Okay," she said quietly. "Let me pack a bag."

Ten minutes later, Cassie came down the stairs with a duffel slung over her shoulder. Her face was pale, her hair still tousled, and her expression unreadable.

"Seth," she asked as they stepped toward the door, "What about the boutique? I can't leave it unsecured like this."

"Baxter's already working with the town police chief," he told her. "They're arranging an officer rotation to keep watch through the night. No one's getting near it."

Cassie nodded slowly. "And Kathryn…Natalie's with her," she said. "She texted me right before this happened. Kathryn was taking something for her anxiety—she's probably zonked out. I'll call her first thing in the morning."

Seth opened the door for her and gently guided her out.

"Right now," Cassie added, her voice softening, "I just want to get some sleep."

He nodded. "You will."

They stepped into the cool night air and walked side-by-side to his truck. He opened the door for her, waited until she was inside, and gave one last glance at the darkened boutique—its broken windows, its broken silence.

Then he climbed in, started the engine, and they drove away together—leaving the sirens, shattered glass, and swirling questions behind.

For now.

The sun was just starting to burn off the morning fog when the smell of sizzling bacon and fresh coffee filled Seth's kitchen. Cassie, hair damp from a quick shower, sat at the table in one of his old flannel shirts, her phone pressed to her ear.

Seth moved easily through the kitchen, flipping pancakes onto a warm plate while eggs fried on the stove.

Cassie's voice was low but steady. "Natalie, I'm fine, I promise. Shaken, yes. But safe. Seth came and got me last night."

Natalie's voice crackled over the line. "I can't believe someone threw *bricks* through the windows. Cass…"

"I know," Cassie said quietly. "It was calculated. Targeted. They left threats for both me and Kathryn."

"I hate that she's not up to speed yet," Natalie muttered. "She's in the shower. But as soon as she's out, I'll tell her everything. We'll meet you at the boutique in about an hour."

"Thanks," Cassie said. "Be safe."

She ended the call and set the phone down, staring at it for a moment before finally lifting her gaze to Seth.

"She and Kathryn will meet me there in an hour."

"Good," he said as he set two plates down. "Eat first. Then I'll drive you over before I head to the ranger station."

Cassie smiled faintly. "Thanks."

They ate in quiet rhythm, a domestic familiarity settling between them like an old quilt pulled from storage. When she finished her coffee, she stood and reached for her bag.

"I'll just grab my things."

Seth picked up the dishes and walked them to the sink. "Cass."

She looked back at him.

"Would you think about just… moving back in? At least until this settles down. I know we've danced around it, but—last night makes it pretty clear. You're in danger."

Cassie paused at the door, hand on the strap of her bag. Her eyes softened.

"I think you're right," she admitted. "It might be best."

Relief flickered across Seth's face, though he masked it with a short nod.

"I'll bring my things this afternoon," she continued. "Shouldn't take long. I'll be home when you get off work."

Home.

The word lingered in the air like a question answered too soon.

Seth pulled the truck up to the curb outside the boutique, the front windows already covered with plywood from the town's emergency board-up crew.

Cassie reached for the handle, then hesitated.

They looked at each other.

A long, quiet look. The kind that said too much and not enough all at once.

"Thanks," she said, voice soft.

"Be careful," he replied.

"I will."

She climbed down from the truck and closed the door gently. He didn't drive off immediately. She stood on the sidewalk, watching him, one hand resting lightly on the duffel bag hanging from her shoulder.

Seth gave her a nod, the ghost of a smile on his lips.

And then he pulled away—while Cassie turned to face the boarded-up boutique, straightened her shoulders, and walked forward.

Cassie stood near the front counter, arms folded tightly across her chest, as the crime scene investigators continued documenting the boutique. One was crouched near the jagged edge of the broken window, placing shards of glass into evidence bags. Another moved silently around the space, snapping photo after photo of the chaos left behind.

The early light filtered in through the boarded sections of the window, casting stripes of shadow across the floor.

A soft knock on the already open door pulled Cassie's attention toward the front.

Natalie stepped in first, her expression tight but composed.

And behind her was Kathryn.

Her eyes were wide, makeup-free for once, and there was something fragile about the way she carried herself—like porcelain with a crack that hadn't quite shattered yet.

Cassie moved toward them. "Hey."

Kathryn didn't speak. She simply stepped forward and took in the scene.

The plywood boards.

The shards of mannequin limbs swept into corners.

The glass countertop that was now covered with evidence bags—and the notes, each one still readable through the transparent plastic.

Natalie gently touched her arm. "They're still going through everything. It'll be a bit before they finish."

Kathryn gave a slight nod and stepped past them.

She approached the counter, slowly, like she was afraid her legs might give out before she got there.

Cassie followed quietly, watching as Kathryn stared down at the threatening messages—one in particular, scrawled in angry black ink.

"This town was better before your heels hit its sidewalks."

For a long time, Kathryn said nothing.

Cassie watched her face, trying to interpret the emotions flitting across it—anger, sadness, fear.

But there was something else, too.

Something *deeper.*

A flicker Cassie couldn't quite name. Something old. Familiar. Private.

"I'm so sorry," Cassie said softly, stepping closer. "This was meant for both of us. But I know what this shop means to you."

Kathryn didn't look away from the notes.

"This place…" she said slowly, her voice thick, "was the one thing I built that Marshall couldn't touch. When everything around me felt too political, too rigid, too tied to his name—I had *this*. My name. My design. My rules."

She finally looked up, eyes glassy but defiant.

"They didn't just throw bricks through a window, Cass. They hit what was *mine*."

Natalie moved beside them and placed a comforting hand on her back.

"We'll catch whoever did this," she said. "I'll print every single name. Every tie. Every whisper. I don't care who they are."

Kathryn nodded, then took a deep breath.

"I'll be fine," she said, mostly to herself. "I just need a minute."

Cassie stepped back to give her space and met Natalie's eyes.

"She's strong," Natalie whispered.

Cassie nodded. "But even steel bends under the right pressure."

They turned to look back at Kathryn—still standing at the counter, one hand resting gently over the edge of the glass.

As though holding herself together through sheer will alone.

28

At Town Hall, Mayor Carrow's face was a mask of calm. But her hands, resting on the podium before the emergency press conference, were curled into tight fists.

"As mayor, I condemn the vandalism at Valley Vogue," she said smoothly. "And I encourage all citizens to remain peaceful, civil, and respectful."

She paused—just long enough.

"And I also want to remind the public that we are dealing with a number of *unconfirmed allegations,* many of which are being handled through the proper legal channels."

Seth stood in the back of the room with Baxter, jaw tight.

"She's getting ahead of it," he muttered.

"She's doing what cornered people do," Baxter replied. "Calling her version of the truth."

Reporters began to murmur as Denise stepped away from the podium.

One raised a hand. "Madam Mayor—are you denying your signature on the Green Horizons documents?"

Denise gave a tight smile.

"I'm not denying anything. I'm simply saying… context matters."

That afternoon, a man in a black suit visited Valley Vogue.

Kathryn was still sweeping glass when he knocked gently on the open front door that displayed the "CLOSED" sign.

"You're closed, I take it?" he asked.

Cassie stepped forward. "Who are you?"

The man handed her a card: Thomas Ainsley, Regional Real Estate Consultant.

"I represent a development group looking to revitalize downtown properties," he said. "We heard about the incident. Thought you might want an out."

Cassie narrowed her eyes. "Let me guess. Green Horizons?"

He smiled faintly. "They go by *Pinewood Capital* now. Same vision, better branding."

Kathryn appeared beside her. "You want me to sell?"

"We're prepared to offer well above market," Ainsley said. "You'll be able to open a boutique anywhere. New York. Atlanta. Somewhere… less tense."

Kathryn stared at him. "Tell Carrow I said go to hell."

He left without another word.

Later that evening, as Cassie and Seth were having dinner, she told him, "The mayor's moving fast, a man offered to buy Valley Vogue today."

Seth's jaw flexed. "She's trying to erase every witness. Every place tied to you."

"Next it'll be me."

Seth turned toward her. "You could leave and go back to Charlotte, Cass, just until this all blows over."

"I won't."

"I know."

They sat in silence for a long moment.

Then Seth added quietly, "But if this goes where I think it's going… we might not all come out clean."

Cassie looked at him. "Would you still stand beside me if it meant giving up your badge?"

He didn't answer right away.

Then, slowly, he nodded.

"For the truth? Yeah. I'd burn the whole damn town down."

Kathryn called a meeting that night in the boutique's back room.

Cassie, Natalie, and Margaret sat around a table, the air heavy with purpose.

"I'm filing an injunction," Kathryn said. "Against the mayor's office and any development deals attached to Green Horizons or its subsidiaries."

Margaret blinked. "You'll have to name her directly."

"I will."

"And you'll paint a target on your back," Natalie added.

"I already have one," Kathryn said. "Might as well make it count."

Cassie reached across the table, resting a hand on hers. "You don't have to do this."

"Yes," Kathryn replied. "I do."

Because if they attacked her shop and expected her to crawl away?

They forgot who she was.

The news hit the town like a lightning strike through dry timber.

A hunter's dog, loose in the lower forest, had uncovered a shallow grave off an unofficial trail near the Wren Hollow ridge.

By sundown, it was confirmed: the body was Tyler Griggs.

Cassie sat in the passenger seat of Baxter's patrol car as they loaded the remains into the coroner's van, her chest tight, jaw clenched.

He hadn't run. He hadn't disappeared.

He had been buried.

Someone had wanted to make sure he stayed hidden.

And now the town had a body.

Now it had blood.

The next morning, Celia Beaumont arrived at Valley Vogue with no warning, wrapped in a soft gray shawl, her silver hair twisted neatly into a braid down her back. She was small, regal, and oddly calm—like someone who'd already survived every storm once before.

Kathryn offered her tea.

Celia declined.

"I don't intend to stay long," she said. "But you need to know something. Before the wrong person tells it their way."

Cassie stood beside the checkout counter, listening closely.

Celia turned toward her.

"You know our family's patriarch, Galen, helped found this town," she said.

Cassie nodded. "Yes. Galen Valley."

"But he didn't do it alone."

Celia reached into her purse and unfolded an old newspaper clipping—preserved in a plastic sleeve, yellowed at the edges.

"*Hollinger Timber Co. Partners with Beaumont Estate to Launch Galen Valley Homestead Project.*"

"The Hollinger family provided the land. Galen provided the vision."

Cassie looked at the faded black-and-white image of two men shaking hands. One was unmistakably Galen Beaumont.

The other—Albert Hollinger—had a smile that didn't quite reach his eyes.

Celia's voice softened. "The Hollingers have always had more power than they let on. They owned the lumber. The mills. The permits. And they controlled the council in the shadows."

Cassie frowned. "They're still around?"

Celia nodded. "Henry Hollinger—Albert's grandson—is now the head of the land commission."

Cassie's heart dropped.

"That includes Wren Hollow."

"Yes," Celia said. "And that includes the failed Green Horizons deal."

At the station, Seth sat with Baxter and the coroner reviewing the initial report.

Tyler had been dead for weeks.

He'd suffered a blow to the head. No gunshot. No defensive wounds. Likely struck from behind.

Whoever did it knew the forest.

Knew the trails.

And knew where to bury a body without anyone stumbling across it.

"This was personal," Seth said quietly.

Baxter didn't argue.

Cassie met Natalie in the back of Everbrew Café and laid out the newspaper clipping beside the latest property logs.

"Henry Hollinger sits on the board of the land commission."

Natalie's eyes narrowed. "And he's one of the investors behind Pinewood Capital. They changed the name but not the money."

"So the Hollingers helped Devon clean his books," Cassie whispered. "And now they're helping Mayor Carrow buy silence."

"Or bury it," Natalie added grimly.

Cassie looked toward the window, her reflection faint in the glass.

"Then it's time the town remembers that not every legacy is worth preserving."

That night, Celia invited Cassie to Sage Manor.

It was the first time Cassie had stepped inside the sprawling estate that bordered the edge of Pisgah National Forest. Warm lighting, old wood, and polished silver framed every room with elegance—but it didn't feel cold.

It felt timeless.

"You're wondering why I'm helping now," Celia said, handing her a thin leather journal.

Cassie nodded. "Yes. I thought the Beaumonts stayed out of this kind of thing."

"We do," Celia said. "Until the silence starts to rot the walls."

Cassie opened the journal.

It was Galen's. Filled with handwritten notes, land sketches, personal letters.

One entry caught her eye:

"Albert wants to bury something. Says the town won't grow unless we all agree to forget. But I don't believe in burying the truth just to build a prettier town square."

Cassie looked up, stunned. "He knew."

"He always did," Celia said. "But he also knew his family couldn't stop the Hollingers alone."

She rested a hand on Cassie's shoulder.

"Maybe yours can."

29

Cassie stared at the old journal page long after Celia Beaumont had left the room. The candle beside her flickered low, casting Galen's handwriting in dancing shadows.

"Albert wants to bury something..."

The Hollinger legacy wasn't just stained.

It was *built* on something rotten. She snapped a photo with her phone and left the manor.

Kathryn was already preparing for war.

She stood in Valley Vogue, clipboard in hand, coordinating with a small but fierce team of supporters—business owners, former council aides, and one retired judge.

"We're filing to block any future Pinewood Capital developments and requesting a formal ethics investigation into Mayor Carrow's financials," she said, her voice low but razor-sharp.

Cassie watched her work and felt something she hadn't felt in a long time.

Hope.

Maybe they could *win.*

At the ranger's station, Seth stood over Marshall's old safe from inside his office, now unsealed and under review. The FBI special agents had cleared most of it—but something had felt off to him. Too clean. Too deliberate.

He checked the inside one last time, tapping the back panel.

It clicked.

He pried it loose and pulled out a hidden folder—inside, printed transcripts of intercepted calls and emails.

And not just about Cassie.

There were logs documenting conversations between *Sheriff Marshall Bowen* and the mayor.

Seth's blood ran cold.

One entry caught his eye:

"MB to DC: 'I'm managing Dixon. He won't step out of line.'"

Seth closed the folder slowly.

Marshall had been keeping him close—not to help and protect him…

But to *control* him.

Cassie was halfway through drafting her exposé on the Hollingers when her phone rang.

Unknown number.

She almost didn't answer.

But something in her gut told her to.

"Cass?"

Elliot.

She stood up fast. "Where are you?"

"Just crossed the county line. I'm coming home."

Cassie blinked. "You said—"

"I know what I said," he cut in. "But you need to hear this in person. I found something. Something I think Tyler was chasing before he died."

Cassie's heart pounded. "What is it?"

"It's not just about the land deals," Elliot said. "It's about the *school*."

Cassie froze. "What?"

"Tyler applied to substitute teach here. He was turned down—fast. Like someone didn't want him in the system. And guess what? One of the board members who blacklisted him... is Henry Hollinger's wife."

Cassie dropped into the nearest chair.

It all looped back.

Control. Money. Legacy.

Even the classrooms weren't safe.

That evening, when Seth came home, he looked shaken.

"You okay?" she asked.

"No," he said quietly. "I found something. Something about Marshall."

Her stomach dropped. "Tell me."

He handed her the folder, watching her face as she read the call transcripts.

Each line stung worse than the last.

"He was playing both sides," Cassie whispered. "He acted like he supported us—like he wanted the truth."

Seth's voice was bitter. "He wanted to *manage* the truth."

She looked up. "What are you going to do?"

Seth hesitated.

"Turn these over to the FBI, let them know they missed them the first time they looked in his safe."

Cassie blinked.

"You sure?"

He nodded. "Of course, I know it makes me look foolish because I trusted Marshall so blindly but this all has to come out."

Cassie stepped closer.

They didn't speak.

But something passed between them.

Respect. Pain. Maybe something deeper.

Whatever it was, it didn't need words.

Not tonight.

The smell of coffee and skillet-fried sausage filled the air as sunlight streamed through the kitchen windows of Seth's house. The morning was quiet, the kind of quiet that felt intentional—earned, almost.

Cassie sat at the table, slowly stirring cream into her coffee. She glanced up at Seth across the table, and then, with a breath, said it.

"I need to tell you something before the day gets away from us."

Seth looked up from his plate. "Okay."

"Elliot called late last night," she said. "It's about the school. There's more going on than we realized, and he said he's found something... damning. Natalie and I are going to meet him this morning to see what he has."

Seth set his fork down.

Cassie rushed gently ahead. "I just want to be completely transparent with you about this. I won't be alone with him. I don't want this to damage what we've started building back here."

She reached across the table, fingers brushing his hand.

"If you want to come with us, I'm okay with that. Truly."

Seth was quiet for a long moment. Then, slowly, he stood.

Cassie looked up at him as he walked around the table and stopped beside her.

He held out a hand.

She took it.

He pulled her up gently and into a tight embrace, his chin resting against her temple.

"Thank you," he said quietly. "For telling me. For not letting me find out some other way."

Cassie's shoulders softened.

Seth pulled back just enough to meet her gaze.

"No," he said. "I'm not going with you. I'm going to trust you. We have to build back on trust, Cass. And you telling me this? That's a step in the right direction. A big one."

She nodded, the tension in her chest loosening.

"Thank you," she whispered.

They held each other for a beat longer, then shared a kiss that was soft but lingering—full of unspoken understanding and something new: stability.

They broke apart with matching half-smiles, and without another word, began clearing the breakfast table, falling into an easy rhythm that felt like old times... but better.

As they each headed for the door—Cassie grabbing her jacket, Seth clipping on his badge—he turned back to her once more.

"Call me when it's over," he said.

"I will."

Then they parted ways into a morning neither of them could yet predict, the next truth waiting just around the corner.

Cassie, Natalie and Elliot sat cross-legged on the apartment floor, a pile of Tyler Griggs's recovered belongings between them. His cracked phone. His field notes. And a flash drive.

It was labeled in black ink: BF.

"Burn file," Elliot muttered. "He left this for someone to find. Maybe even you."

Natalie plugged it into her laptop and waited.

Inside: six folders. Photos. Documents. Screenshots. Emails. Two labeled audio files.

She opened the first.

Tyler's voice crackled through.

"If you're hearing this, I probably didn't make it out. Hollinger controls the land. But the town? That's Carrow. And she doesn't just hide things—she buries them. Start with the purchase orders. Look for Pinewood, Cypress West, and anything tied to 'educational grants.' It's how they clean the money."

Natalie opened the folder marked EDUCATION.

Inside were PDFs from the town's school board budget. A pattern emerged fast.

Three "community education enrichment" grants had been issued in the past five years—all to shell foundations connected to Cypress West.

One name kept appearing in the approval signatures:

Eleanor Hollinger.

Henry Hollinger's wife.

Board member.

And the woman who'd blocked Tyler's application to substitute teach. The same woman who had led the board in pressuring Elliot about his relationship with Cassie.

Cassie's heart pounded.

"They used the schools," she said. "To launder the money."

"And to keep people like Tyler out," Elliot added.

30

At the ranger's station, Seth entered the cell block where Marshall was still being held.

He stood right outside the door of his cell. Marshall didn't look up.

"Are you going to pretend I am not standing here?" Seth said.

"Not much to say, I have a right to remain silent."

"True, so I guess you can just listen then. I found the secret compartment in your safe."

Marshall sighed. Hung his head lower.

"I *read* what you said to the mayor."

Marshall's jaw tightened. "I was trying to protect you."

"By managing me? By lying to me?"

"You weren't ready to know everything, Seth."

Seth's voice was ice. "Try me."

Marshall finally looked at him. "There's more at stake than you understand. The Hollingers have ties in state government. You bring them down, you bring the whole damn town down with them."

"Then maybe it needs to fall."

Marshall stood. "You don't know what you're saying."

Seth shook his head. "Maybe not, after all I allowed you to make me look like a fool but never again."

Seth turned and walked out knowing he would never lay eyes on Marshall again. The special agents planned to move him to a Raleigh detention center the next morning.

Seth had to confront him, and needed to see Marshall's reaction to what Seth had found.

Now he had it.

Natalie clicked *Publish* at 10:12 a.m.

Her article was simple, powerful, and blistering.

"From Timber to Tyranny: How a Founding Family Turned a Quiet Town Into a Money Laundering Haven."

The names were all there.

Devon Blake.

Henry and Eleanor Hollinger.

Denise Carrow.

The school board.

The development firms.

The real estate shell companies.

The piece exploded within minutes.

By noon, it had trended nationally.

By 3 p.m., reporters descended on Galen Valley.

Cassie stepped out onto her porch as the first camera crew arrived at the end of her driveway. She didn't wave. Didn't hide.

She stood tall.

Natalie joined her, handing her a coffee.

"You okay?"

"No," she said honestly. "But I'm ready."

From behind them, Seth pulled up in his truck.

He stepped out, holding a manila envelope.

"What's that?" she asked.

He handed it to her.

"My statement."

Cassie's breath caught. "What?"

"I'm planning to bust this wide open using the full weight of my position."

She opened the envelope.

Inside was his statement—signed and notarized—detailing everything he'd witnessed working alongside the sheriff department during the Tyler Griggs investigation.

A full confession.

And a promise to testify.

Cassie looked up at him. "You know this makes you a target."

He gave a tired smile. "I was already a target the moment I stood next to you."

The town was watching now.

Not whispering.

Watching.

And Cassie wasn't running.

She was leading. And Seth was right beside her.

It started with smoke.

A soft gray curl rising behind Valley Vogue, slipping through the cool night air like a whisper.

Then came the flames.

By the time Cassie and Seth reached the scene, the fire had devoured half the boutique.

Kathryn stood on the curb, barefoot, wearing only a robe and sheer disbelief, her hands clenched in fists at her sides. Natalie was with her, still in her pajamas.

"It was the back entrance," she said quietly. "Someone broke the lock."

Cassie rushed to her, wrapping an arm around her shoulders as firefighters moved in with axes and hoses, their shouts breaking the otherwise stunned silence.

"They couldn't shut us up or buy me out," Kathryn murmured, voice raw. "So they tried to burn us down."

Cassie didn't say anything.

Because she knew it was true.

Elliot arrived minutes later, still in jeans and an old T-shirt, his hair wild with sleep and panic.

"Are you okay?" he asked Kathryn and Cassie.

"We're alive," Kathryn said. "That's more than they wanted."

The fire was ruled arson before sunrise.

No security footage.

No fingerprints.

Just a single line of graffiti left behind on the alley wall—red spray paint, barely legible through the smoke.

"BURN WITH YOUR TRUTH."

By noon, the story had gone national.

Footage of the blaze played in a split-screen beside Natalie's exposé. Anchors used words like *"retaliation," "corruption,"* and *"a modern Salem."*

Cassie stared at the screen in silence.

Then her phone rang.

An unknown number again.

She answered anyway.

"Mrs. Dixon?" the voice on the other end was calm, polished. "This is Kate Morales, senior producer for *The National Ledger*. We'd like to fly you to New York. Prime-time segment. Full interview. We want you to tell your story—your *whole* story."

Cassie blinked. "Why now?"

"Because you're not just news anymore," Morales said. "You're a *movement.*"

Later that day, Natalie and Cassie sat with Kathryn at her kitchen table, the smoke of the destroyed boutique still clinging to their skin.

"You going to take it?" Natalie asked.

She didn't answer right away.

"I don't want to be a symbol," she said. "I just wanted peace."

"Too late for peace," Kathryn said. "But maybe it's not too late for purpose."

Cassie looked at her, eyes heavy with everything they'd survived.

"If I do this," she said slowly, "I can't stop halfway. I have to name everyone. Even the ones who didn't throw matches but stood and watched it burn."

"Then name them," Kathryn said. "And let the world see the fire."

Seth came home that evening with a flash drive in hand.

"What's this?" Cassie asked.

"Everything from Marshall's archives," he said. "Hidden files. Off-the-book conversations. Reports that never made it to evidence."

Cassie stared at it.

"I don't know where this ends," she whispered.

Seth's voice was calm. "Then make sure it ends with *you.* Not them."

At the edge of town, Denise Carrow sat in her darkened office, the flickering light of the news broadcast dancing across her whiskey glass.

They had gone further than she expected.

And they weren't backing down.

She picked up her phone and dialed a private number.

"It's me. Pull the trigger on the asset transfer. If she goes on national TV... we'll need to move fast."

She paused.

"And find out where Beaumont stands. I don't trust her silence."

That night, Cassie stood outside the charred remains of Valley Vogue with Kathryn and Natalie.

Smoke still clung to the sidewalk.

But behind it, something brighter stirred.

Resolve.

Rage.

Clarity.

No one was going to save Galen Valley.

Not the police.

Not the press.

Not the ghosts of the founding families.

Only the truth could.

And she was ready to set it free.

31

The fire had barely cooled when the news hit: Marshall Bowen was found dead.

Hung himself in his jail cell at the ranger's station.

Must have been the weight of the secrets and lies. The years of walking the line between protector and puppet that made him do it.

He'd watched too long. Gotten too deep into the corruption.

And it had eaten him from the inside out.

Seth stood back as they rolled the gurney out with the lifeless body of Sheriff Marshall Bowen, covered by a sheet that matched the one he had hung himself with.

Kathryn stood beside him in the silence. She hadn't cried. Hadn't flinched. She watched the exit as if waiting for something else—some truth or memory—to follow behind the body.

But nothing came.

Seth cleared his throat gently, speaking low. "We're transferring the body to the local funeral home. They'll hold him there until arrangements are made."

Kathryn finally turned to him, her face unreadable.

"Thank you, Seth," she said. "But there won't be any arrangements."

Seth blinked. "You don't want a service?"

"No," she said firmly, crossing her arms. "Marshall didn't want one. Told me years ago—if anything ever happened to him, he didn't want speeches or ceremonies. Just... ashes buried somewhere out near the hunting cabin. That's where he found peace. Out in those trees."

Seth nodded slowly, respectfully. "Do you need help coordinating the cremation? I can make a call to—"

"I've already handled it," she interrupted gently. "Spoke with a director I trust. Quiet and quick. No programs. No guest list. Just me and whatever's left of the man I married, walking into the woods one last time."

Seth's throat tightened, but he didn't argue.

"I appreciate your offer," she added, voice softening, "but this part... I need to do alone."

He looked at her carefully. "Are you sure?"

Kathryn glanced toward the exit, where Marshall's body had disappeared moments before.

"Marshall was a complicated man. Most people only ever saw the polished version. The badge. The charm. The politics." She paused, then met Seth's gaze again. "I saw the rest."

Seth swallowed hard. "If there's anything you need—after—"

"I know where to find you," she said.

Then she turned and walked away down the hallway, her heels echoing behind her like the last line of a closing chapter.

Seth stood there for another long minute, alone with the silence.

And the weight of everything that had been left unsaid.

The east parlor at Sage Manor was bathed in golden light, its velvet drapes pulled halfway back as the sun slanted through the tall, arched windows. Cassie sat stiffly on the edge of a brocade settee, hands wrapped around a cup of chamomile tea she hadn't touched.

Across from her, Celia Beaumont folded her hands gently in her lap, her expression calm but alert.

"I still can't believe it," Cassie murmured. "Marshall... gone like that."

Celia nodded slowly, her gaze flickering toward the window. "Grief wears many faces, but shame… shame tends to choose silence."

Cassie looked down at her cup. "I should've never dragged Kathryn into any of this. I thought I was helping—with her social media, marketing for the boutique—but I only led her deeper into a mess she didn't deserve."

Celia's eyes sharpened.

"No," she said softly but firmly. "You didn't drag her in, Cassie. She was already *in*. Courtesy of the man she married."

Cassie looked up.

"Marshall had secrets," Celia continued. "We all suspected it. Some of us even knew a few. But Kathryn… she didn't know how deep they went. Not until you started uncovering what was buried. What *he* buried."

"But it broke her," Cassie whispered. "She's unraveling."

"She's grieving," Celia corrected gently. "But grief doesn't mean broken. You didn't cause this. You simply *revealed* it."

Cassie blinked back the sting in her eyes and nodded slowly, letting Celia's words settle in.

A long pause followed before Celia tilted her head slightly.

"But you didn't come here just to talk about Kathryn."

Cassie sat back, exhaling slowly. "No. I didn't."

Celia's brow lifted. "Then tell me what's weighing on you."

Cassie hesitated, then reached into her bag and pulled out a thin folder—worn at the corners from being handled again and again. She set it gently on the table between them.

"There's something happening in Galen Valley," she said. "Something *old*. Something that's rooted deeper than I think any of us realized."

Celia's eyes dropped to the folder, then back to Cassie.

"And you think I know where the roots begin."

Cassie nodded. "I think the answers start here. In this house. With your family."

Celia was quiet for a long moment, her gaze thoughtful, unreadable.

Then she stood and crossed the parlor slowly, her heels soundless against the aged rugs.

She stopped beside a tall hutch, opened a hidden latch, and withdrew an aged wooden box—its corners worn smooth by time, the latch faintly tarnished.

She carried it with reverence to the mantle and placed it down gently.

Then, she lit a tall white candle beside it.

She hadn't touched the box in decades.

Cassie stood across from her, unsure whether to sit or speak.

Celia opened the box slowly, revealing a bundle of letters tied with silk ribbon and a heavy silver key.

"This belonged to Galen," she said quietly. "He kept it in his study until the day he died. He left instructions to never give it to anyone unless they believed the town couldn't be saved without it."

Cassie's breath hitched. "And now you do?"

Celia's eyes didn't waver. "Now I *know*."

She passed the bundle to Cassie.

Inside the letters: correspondence between Galen Beaumont and Albert Hollinger, spanning decades.

One stood out.

"Albert—

What you did on that land was not just unethical. It was a crime. One you've covered with favors, gifts, and fear. You told me it was a mistake. I no longer believe that. I will not sign off on the second easement until you come clean. This town is not your hiding place. It is our home. And we owe it more than this."

Cassie's hands trembled as she read it again.

Galen Beaumont knew.

And he *refused* to be part of the cover-up.

Celia opened a small compartment at the bottom of the box and handed Cassie a worn manila envelope.

Inside: a map.

The original hand-drawn layout of the town—annotated with symbols, markers, and an entire quadrant labeled "disputed grounds."

It matched the coordinates where Tyler Griggs had been found.

"They buried him where the *first body* was buried," Celia said.

Cassie looked up, stunned. "What first body?"

"An investigative journalist," Celia whispered. "Back decades ago. Asking the wrong questions. Galen suspected Albert had him killed. But no proof. No charges. The man just vanished."

Cassie sat back, reeling.

"This is… *everything.*"

Celia nodded. "Then take it. And make sure it's never buried again."

Cassie's flight to New York was scheduled for the next morning.

Seth drove her to the airport, neither of them speaking much on the drive. They didn't need to.

As they pulled into the lot, he finally asked:

"You ready?"

Cassie looked out at the mountains in the distance.

"No," she said. "But I'm going anyway."

He smiled softly. "Good. Because the world's finally ready to listen."

Back in Galen Valley, the mayor received an envelope.

No return address.

Inside: a copy of Galen Beaumont's letter to Albert Hollinger.

And a post-it note:

"The ghosts are coming. And they're bringing receipts."

32

The lights were blinding.

Cassie sat on the cushioned interview set across from *The National Ledger's* anchor, Vanessa Holt—a woman with sharp eyes and an even sharper reputation.

Her heart pounded like a drum, but her voice remained steady as cameras rolled and the red light blinked to life.

Vanessa smiled. "Cassie Dixon, thank you for being here. I think it's fair to say the entire country is watching Galen Valley right now. Why speak out now?"

Cassie inhaled slowly.

"Because I tried silence. I tried hiding. And all that did was give other people time to build a narrative that wasn't true."

Vanessa leaned forward. "And what is the truth?"

Cassie unfolded Galen's letter on the table between them.

"The truth is that this town was built on a lie. And people have died to keep that lie alive."

Back in Galen Valley, the town came to a near standstill.

Televisions in cafés, diners, offices—even the sheriff's station—were tuned in. Some people watched with mouths slightly open, stunned.

Others cursed under their breath.

Mayor Denise Carrow sat in her office, glass of wine in hand, a flicker of panic creeping into her perfectly smooth expression.

Because Cassie hadn't come with claims.

She came with *evidence.*

Letters. Maps. Emails. Scans. Recordings.

"The cover-up didn't start with me," Cassie said, voice steady through the broadcast. "It started long before. Before the nonprofit. Before the school funding. Before the fires. Before Tyler Griggs. This town has had secrets buried under the pines for generations."

And then she named names.

The Hollingers.

The mayor.

The shell companies.

The board members.

The silent protectors.

She never raised her voice.

She didn't need to.

Because this time, the receipts spoke louder than she ever could.

Kathryn, Natalie, and Seth watched together from Kathyrn's living room. It was awkward for Seth at first seeing all of the photos of Marshall sitting around the home but Kathryn put him at ease. He felt as though Kathryn had handled Marshall's death better than his arrest.

He was glad to see the many floral arrangements and plants scattered around the house that had been sent to her during her grieving the loss of her husband.

Kathryn exhaled. "She did it. Seth, I know you are proud of her, I know I am."

Natalie nodded, stunned. "She didn't just drop a bomb. She lit a match and *named the flame.*"

Seth didn't say anything for a moment.

Then: "Now we hold the line."

Cassie sat near Gate 12, her carry-on tucked beneath the seat and her phone pressed to her ear. The terminal buzzed around her with the low hum of rolling luggage, boarding announcements, and conversations, but all she focused on was the voice on the other end of the line.

"Okay," she said, almost shyly. "Be honest. How did I do?"

On the other end, Seth leaned against the brick wall of Kathryn's house, one boot propped against it, phone to his ear. They had stepped out on her front porch for some fresh air after the broadcast had finished.

"You were incredible," he said without hesitation. "Strong. Smart. Composed. You didn't just show them who you are—you reminded *us* who you are."

Cassie exhaled slowly, letting the words wrap around her like a warm coat.

Kathryn's voice came faintly in the background through speakerphone: "You made the whole town proud, sweetheart."

Then Natalie: "Even the people who pretend not to be watching? They're watching now."

Cassie laughed softly, her tension slowly unwinding. "Thank you. All of you. Now we wait for the public fallout, right?"

Seth's tone softened. "We're ready for it."

Cassie looked at the clock above the gate. "My flight's still on time, by some miracle. I've got a layover in Charlotte, so I'll call you from there. Should give you enough time to head to Asheville to pick me up."

"I'll be there," Seth said. "Early. You know I hate airport traffic."

"I do," she smiled. "And I appreciate it anyway."

There was a pause, a silence that hummed with something more than just connection.

Seth stepped off the porch and into the yard, seeking a little more quiet.

"I'm really proud of you, Cass," he said, voice low. "You faced everything they threw at you. And now you're coming back stronger."

"I couldn't have done any of this without you," she said as her voice wavered just slightly.

His voice thickened. "I can't wait to have you back *at* home."

"I miss you," she said simply.

"I miss you too."

Over the intercom, her flight began boarding.

"That's me," she said, rising from her seat.

"Call me from Charlotte."

"I will."

They didn't need a long goodbye.

Just a quiet one.

"Bye, Seth."

"Bye, Cassie."

She ended the call and stood there for a moment, smiling to herself.

And as she joined the boarding line, the nerves didn't come.

Only resolve.

That night, as the interview trended online and news trucks began descending on Galen Valley, Denise Carrow met with Henry Hollinger behind the locked doors of town hall.

"You said she wouldn't talk," Henry growled.

"She didn't have proof," Denise snapped.

"She *does now*."

Henry poured a drink with shaking hands. "Then we end this. Tonight."

But the town had already heard the truth.

And it believed Cassie.

33

Cassie woke up wrapped in Seth's arms. Their subdued reunion at the airport has blossomed into a more intimate one once they arrived back at the house.

Once he left for work, she decided to lay back down and try to catch up on sleep but her laptop kept dinging with notifications, she opened it up to find her inbox was flooded.

Messages from strangers thanking her. From reporters begging for more interviews. From survivors of other towns who had lived in silence far too long.

She answered none of them.

Instead, she called Kathryn to check in on her. Kathryn said she too was still at home contemplating her next steps with Valley Vogue.

Cassie pulled into Kathryn's driveway, stepped onto the porch and knocked once.

Kathryn opened the door wearing leggings, a cozy sweater, and no shoes, a steaming cup of coffee already in hand.

"Told you I was staying home today," she smiled, stepping aside to let Cassie in.

Cassie followed her to the kitchen, where sunlight spilled across the oak table and the smell of cinnamon lingered faintly in the air. A second mug waited for her, still hot.

They sat down across from each other, the clink of ceramic breaking the silence first.

Kathryn took one sip, then tilted her head. "Something's different about you."

Cassie blinked. "Different?"

Kathryn's eyes narrowed, playful but suspicious. "New makeup? You're positively *glowing.*"

Cassie grinned. "Nope. I'm not wearing any makeup at all today. Maybe it's just the way the sun is beaming in?"

Kathryn leaned closer, squinting like a detective. "Oh no, that's not a glow from the sun. That's either expertly blended foundation and highlighter or..."

Cassie raised an eyebrow.

Kathryn smirked. "A happy morning after."

Cassie blushed instantly. "Kathryn!"

Kathryn sat back, victorious. "Mmmhmm. That's what I thought."

Cassie laughed into her coffee, shaking her head. "Okay, fine. Yes. Me and Seth... we're figuring it out. And I can honestly say—I'm happy. Still scared, obviously. Everything with the town, the investigation, all the eyes on me... But with Seth?"

She placed her hand over her chest. "That part? Feels good. Feels *right.*"

Kathryn's smile softened. "Cassie, I can't think of two people I'm happier to see working it out. You deserve good things. Don't talk yourself out of them."

Cassie nodded, touched by the sincerity in her friend's voice.

Kathryn set her mug down and stood. "Speaking of things you deserve..." She crossed the kitchen, grabbed her purse from the counter, and pulled out a small envelope tied in a faded green ribbon.

She returned to the table and gently slid it across to Cassie.

"What's this?" Cassie asked, already loosening the ribbon.

"Celia Beaumont dropped it off for you," Kathryn said. "Said it was something personal. Asked me to make sure you got it directly."

Cassie's fingers stilled for a moment on the envelope flap.

"Did she say anything else?"

Kathryn shook her head. "Just that you'd understand what to do with it when the time was right."

Cassie's heart thudded softly in her chest.

She opened the envelope and pulled out a handwritten letter to her from Celia along with a folded piece of parchment paper.

Dearest Cassie,

This is a Hollinger ledger that Galen kept hidden for years. It was how Albert managed his debts—quietly. He used coded initials, but I think you'll recognize a few.

Warmest Regards,

Celia

Cassie opened the ledger slowly, scanning the first page.

And there it was:

"Loan settlement to D.C.—facilitated through CWC account. Collateral: Sage Hill parcel."

Her mouth went dry as she mumbled, "He sold part of the Beaumont land… to pay off Denise? That can't be her initials, she is not old enough. Who could D.C. be from that timeframe?"

"What are you asking?," Kathryn said.

"Oh, sorry Kathryn." Cassie replied to her as she slid the parchment over for Kathryn to see. "I am perplexed by this ledger Celia has given to me. I need to find out who D.C. could be. The first person that came to mind was Denise Carrow but that's impossible. She would have been born way after this land deal."

"Then maybe you should look into her daddy," Kathryn stated as she took a sip of her coffee. "Marshall ran for Sheriff only after Dawson Carrow decided to finally retire. He was Sheriff for decades."

"Wow," said Cassie stunned by this revelation, "the family connections in this town just never end."

Across town, Denise Carrow sat in her office with two lawyers and a freshly poured glass of bourbon, the curtain drawn tight against the growing presence of journalists outside.

"You've lost the public," one of the lawyers said bluntly. "And if even half the financial trail is verified, you're looking at multiple charges."

"We need to discuss your resignation," the other added.

Denise didn't answer right away.

Instead, she opened the bottom drawer of her desk and pulled out a black velvet jewelry box.

Inside: a gold medallion with the Carrow family crest.

"My family and I have given this town everything," she whispered. "I buried secrets for them. I built roads that bear my family's name. I *kept the lights on.*"

She closed the box gently.

"And now they want to watch me fall."

Seth received the call at 2:47 p.m.

Unknown number. Just a voice.

"She's gone."

He froze. "Who?"

"Cassie Dixon."

Then the line went dead.

It wasn't true.

Not yet.

But it was enough to panic him.

He called Cassie—no answer. Drove straight to Valley Vogue—empty. Checked the boutique's backdoor and alley.

Nothing.

Then finally, as he raced toward Kathryn's house in desperation, his phone buzzed.

Cassie.

He answered on the first ring.

"Where the hell are you?"

"I'm okay," she said breathlessly. "I am at Kathryn's. My phone died."

Seth exhaled shakily and pulled over.

"Someone just called me and said you'd disappeared."

"Probably meant to scare you," Cassie said. "They're getting desperate."

Seth's jaw clenched. "Or they're getting *ready.*"

But the town was already spiraling.

As more journalists entered the town and started asking questions about Cassie's television interview, more residents found out about the corruption and became upset. They formed protests outside Town Hall and waved signs. Stores began pulling donations and support from Pinewood Capital.

And then—like an ember hitting dry brush—another match was lit.

A reporter from *The Daily Standard* published a leaked federal arrest warrant draft.

Apparently Marshall had talked before he committed suicide.

It named Denise Carrow, Henry Hollinger, his wife Eleanor, and two former school board officials.

The town gasped.

But Denise didn't wait to be arrested.

She held a press conference that evening—hair curled, pearls in place, voice like lacquered steel.

"I have no intention of resigning," she said calmly. "I will fight every accusation. I have done nothing wrong and I will not apologize for protecting the legacy of this town from chaos."

Cassie watched the broadcast from Kathryn's home, her jaw tight.

"She's going to try to outlast this," she muttered.

Kathryn scoffed. "Not on *my* watch. I am going down there tomorrow morning. We have lost confidence in our mayor and she has to resign or be removed. I think I can round up the votes to accomplish that."

But by nightfall, chaos arrived anyway.

Natalie was gone. She always came over in the evening to stay the night with Kathryn and when she did not arrive, Kathryn called Seth and Cassie.

"Something's wrong," Kathryn told them, "Natalie normally comes for dinner and stays the night then goes back to her hotel room to work for the day."

"Double check your phone to make sure you have not received any missed phone calls or text messages," Cassie asked Kathryn.

"Nothing," Kathryn said, "I already did that."

"Ok, sit tight," Cassie told her, "keep your doors locked. Seth and I will drive to the hotel to check on her."

Arriving at the hotel, Natalie's car was in the parking lot, the hotel door pushed open when they knocked on it and her laptop was sitting open on the small desk. Nothing looked plundered or askew.

"It does not look like there has been a struggle in here," Seth told Cassie, "but I don't have a good feeling about this."

"Maybe she went to dinner with Elliot before he leaves town and just lost track of time," Cassie said, "I'm going to give him a call."

"Ok," Seth replied, "I am calling Baxter to give him a heads up we may have another missing person, my gut tells me she is not with Elliot."

34

As Cassie waited for Elliot to respond to her phone call and text message, she took a closer look at Natalie's laptop. It was open to a draft article titled:

"What Happened to Marshall Bowen?"

But the article was half-written.

Natalie wouldn't have walked away without finishing it.

And she sure as hell wouldn't have left without locking her door.

Seth and Cassie stood in the middle of the hotel room, tension thick in the air. He was waiting to hear back from Baxter and she was waiting on Elliot.

Suddenly she noticed something else, Natalie's phone! It was lying on the bed partially hidden by the bedding. Cassie's hands trembled as she picked it up. It was still plugged into the charger.

Now she really did fear something terrible has happened to Natalie, she most definitely would not have left without her phone.

Seth removed it from the charger to take a closer look.

No recent calls.

No recent messages.

Except one unsent text to Cassie:

"I think I know who..."

That was it.

The sentence stopped mid-thought.

No name.

No explanation.

Just the start of a revelation cut short.

The air in the hotel room was heavy with tension.

Seth paced slowly near the door, his phone in hand, glancing down every few seconds as if willing it to ring.

"She was supposed to be at Kathryn's by now," Cassie said quietly, still staring out.

"Whatever happened," Seth replied. "she didn't leave on her own."

Cassie swallowed, her voice shaking. "I agree, she would not have left without locking her door and taking her phone."

"We are losing valuable time just standing around," Seth said. "Where is Baxter?"

He dialed Baxter again and left another message. "Call me the second you get this. I need to file a missing person's report."

Cassie turned around, arms still tightly crossed. "You really think she might have been kidnapped?"

"I don't know," Seth said, "something happened that is not normal with her car, phone and laptop just left here like this. Then the door being ajar…none of those are good signs."

Just then, Cassie's phone rang.

Elliot.

She answered immediately, putting the call on speaker. "Elliot? Is Natalie with you?"

"No," Elliot said, his voice tight with concern. "I haven't seen her since yesterday afternoon. Why, what's wrong? You sound upset."

Cassie wanted to confirm. "You haven't heard from her at all today?"

"Not a word," Elliot replied. "I thought she was just laying low while working on her articles. You're telling me she's missing?"

"She's gone," Seth said. "But her stuff's here. Laptop, phone, everything. Her car is in the parking lot."

Elliot went silent.

Cassie said, "She wouldn't disappear. Not without saying something."

"I'm heading over," Elliot said quickly. "Be right there."

Cassie ended her call as Seth redialed Baxter.

This time, he picked up.

"Ross."

"Natalie Oliver is missing," Seth said without preamble. "I'm at her hotel room now with Cassie. Her phone, her laptop, her car—everything's here. But Natalie is not."

Baxter's voice hardened. "You think it's foul play?"

Seth's tone dropped. "Yeah. I do."

"I'll be there in ten," Baxter said. "Bringing two deputies with me. Lock the room down. No one in or out until we get there."

Seth hung up, his face grim as he looked at Cassie.

"She didn't run," Cassie said quietly. "She found something. Something too close to the truth."

Seth nodded. "And someone wanted to shut her up before she could tell it."

They stood in the center of the small hotel room, surrounded by everything that made up Natalie's life in Galen Valley—except for Natalie herself.

And this time, the silence wasn't heavy with tension.

It was heavy with fear.

Darkness.

It swallowed everything—sight, time, sense.

Natalie stirred, her head lolling forward before jerking upright again with a painful throb at the base of her skull. The air was cold and stale, tinged with damp wood and something metallic. Her wrists were bound behind her back, tied tightly to the arms of a chair, her ankles similarly restrained to the legs.

Panic surged as she tried to move, but the bindings were tight—too tight—cutting into her skin every time she flexed.

She froze, trying to breathe through the rising terror.

Where am I? What happened?

She searched her memory.

She'd been in her hotel room. Organizing files. Working on her article. She was texting Cassie about it. A knock at the door. That was the last thing she remembered—a knock.

God, I answered it. I actually opened the door...without asking who it was or looking to see who it was...

Her head throbbed again, a dull, rhythmic ache that made her nauseous.

She shifted slightly, testing her bonds. The chair creaked beneath her, old and unsteady, but solid enough to hold her. Rope, not zip ties. Rough. Coarse. Someone had taken their time.

The floor beneath her feet felt like concrete.

There were no windows. No ambient light. Just the faint echo of dripping water somewhere distant. A basement? A cellar? She couldn't tell.

But she was underground. She felt it in her bones.

Her breathing quickened.

Okay, okay... think.

She rotated her wrists slightly. The rope scraped her skin, but she felt a little give. Not much—but maybe enough.

She swallowed hard, throat dry. "Help," she croaked, then louder. "Help!"

Nothing.

No footsteps. No movement. No voices.

Her eyes burned with the effort to adjust to the darkness. But there was nothing to see. Just pitch black.

She forced herself to inhale deeply.

Then she did the only thing left to do: she prayed.

Please let them know I'm missing. Please let Cassie and Kathryn know. Please let someone get to me before... before they decide to finish whatever this is.

A tear slipped down her cheek, and she angrily shook it off.

She wasn't giving up.

Not yet.

With every ounce of strength, Natalie twisted her wrists, biting back a cry as the rope dug in deeper.

Keep going, she told herself. *Keep moving. They'll come for me. They have to.*

In the darkness, Natalie pulled against her restraints and waited for the smallest crack of light—

And hoped it would come *before it was too late.*

The flashing red and blue lights of the sheriff's department cruisers lit up the small parking lot as deputies arrived and secured the perimeter of the hotel. Cassie stood on the curb outside the room, arms wrapped around herself despite the mild temperature.

Moments later, three vehicles pulled in one after the other—Baxter Ross, a second set of deputies, and Elliot, who climbed out of his car visibly shaken, running a hand through his hair.

Seth met Baxter near the walkway. "We haven't touched anything since we found her stuff. Her phone, laptop, and car are all still here. But no Natalie."

Baxter nodded sharply. "Alright, everyone, I need you to stay outside and stay clear while we secure the room and begin processing the scene. No one enters again until I say so. This is now a crime scene."

Cassie exchanged a worried glance with Seth, then Elliot, before they silently stepped back from the doorway, letting Baxter and the deputies move past them with gloves and evidence kits.

Cassie's phone buzzed in her hand.

Kathryn.

She quickly stepped away from the others and answered. "Hey."

"How bad is it?" Kathryn asked immediately, her voice tight.

Cassie didn't try to soften the blow. "She's missing. Her phone, car, and laptop are here—but she's gone. The deputies and Baxter just arrived. They're processing the scene now, looking for any clues."

There was silence on the other end. Then Kathryn exhaled shakily. "Oh God. What can I do?"

"Right now?" Cassie said gently. "Lock your doors. Set your alarm. Keep your phone close. And don't open the door for *anyone* you don't know. Just stay alert, okay?"

"I will," Kathryn promised. "Keep me posted."

"I will."

Cassie ended the call and turned to rejoin Seth and Elliot, who were standing together near the curb.

"Any updates?" she asked quietly.

Seth shook his head. "Not yet. But Baxter said he needs to talk to you."

Cassie nodded grimly and stepped back toward the open hotel room door, stopping just at the threshold.

"Baxter," she called gently, "you have questions for me?"

He turned away from the desk where he'd been photographing Natalie's laptop and joined her near the doorway, scribbling in a small notepad as he approached.

"Yes," he said. "Thanks for sticking around. I already talked to Elliot."

Cassie folded her arms. "What do you need to know?"

"When's the last time you saw Natalie in person?"

Cassie thought. "Two days ago. Before I left for my interview in New York. We texted briefly last night—but I haven't seen or spoken to her directly."

Baxter jotted that down. "So not today?"

"No. Not at all."

"Who else saw her this morning?"

Cassie's eyes lit with realization. "Kathryn. Natalie was staying at her house last night. She left early this morning. Kathryn may be the last person to have seen her."

Baxter nodded. "I'll send two deputies to her place now. See if she remembers anything—someone Natalie mentioned meeting, a strange car outside, anything."

"Even something small could matter," Cassie added. "She might not realize what she knows."

"Exactly."

Baxter glanced back into the room, then at his deputies beginning to dust for prints on the doorframe.

"We're treating this as a possible abduction," he said, voice low. "And we're not wasting time."

Cassie gave a single, tight nod. "Good."

35

The knock at the door startled Kathryn, though she'd been expecting it since Cassie's phone call. She pulled her cardigan tighter around her and peeked through the side window before unlocking the door.

Two uniformed deputies stood on her porch, one older with a clipboard, the other young and fresh-faced but serious.

"Mrs. Bowen?" the older one asked gently.

"Yes, come in," Kathryn said, stepping aside. "Cassie told me you'd be coming."

They entered, hats tucked respectfully under their arms, and followed her to the living room where she motioned for them to sit. Kathryn remained standing.

"We'll try to be brief," the senior deputy began. "We're gathering a timeline and any details that might help us locate Ms. Oliver. You said she was staying here with you last night?"

"Yes," Kathryn said, folding her arms. "She's been staying here nightly for a few days now."

"And why was that?" the younger deputy asked.

Kathryn gave a tight smile, laced with exhaustion. "Because she's a good friend. After the boutique fire… and Marshall's death…" She hesitated, her throat tightening. "Let's just say I haven't exactly felt safe or particularly grounded. Natalie insisted on staying here to help. I didn't fight her on it."

The older deputy nodded. "When did she leave the house this morning?"

196

"Just after eight. She had coffee, packed her laptop bag, and said she had a lot of research to do."

"Did she mention meeting anyone?"

Kathryn shook her head. "No. Nothing specific. No appointments, no interviews."

The younger deputy leaned forward slightly. "Was there anything unusual this morning? Anything she said or something you saw?"

Kathryn paused, thinking.

"She mentioned needing to dig into something sensitive," she finally said. "She didn't say what, just that she had to finish piecing things together before she told Cassie about it."

"Anything else? Any unusual cars or people in the neighborhood recently?"

Kathryn nodded slowly. "Yes. There's been a black SUV that's shown up a few times over the last few days. Natalie and I even commented on it—wondering if a neighbor had gotten a new car or if it was someone watching us. It always seemed to be parked just far enough away not to raise alarm, but close enough to feel like a shadow."

Both deputies exchanged a quick look.

"Do you remember the make or license plate?"

"I don't," Kathryn admitted. "But it was newer. Tinted windows. Black on black. Natalie mentioned seeing a vehicle like it near the campground a couple of days ago, too."

"That's helpful," the older deputy said. "We'll check traffic cams and street footage in both areas, see what we can find."

Kathryn sighed. "I just... I don't understand how this could happen. She was right here. She was safe."

The younger deputy stood. "We'll do everything we can to find her, ma'am."

She nodded, voice steady despite her fear. "Please do."

As they left, Kathryn closed the door behind them and leaned against it, hand trembling slightly on the knob as she locked back up and set her alarm.

The flashing cruiser lights had dimmed, and most of the sheriff's department vehicles were now parked silently along the hotel lot perimeter. The air had grown colder and a biting breeze swept through the lot as the two deputies that had spoken with Kathryn stepped out of their cruiser and crossed the parking lot toward Baxter.

"Ross," the senior deputy said, "Just got back from Kathryn Bowen's house. She gave us something. Might be a lead."

Baxter looked up from the crime scene log. "Go on."

"She and Natalie had both noticed a black SUV hanging around her neighborhood the past few days. Tinted windows. Parked a few doors down more than once."

Baxter narrowed his eyes. "Black SUV?"

"Yeah," he confirmed. "Newer model. Same kind of thing Natalie apparently saw near the campground a few days ago too."

Baxter's stomach dropped.

"The boutique," he muttered.

The deputies looked confused.

Baxter snapped the crime log shut and turned abruptly, striding toward the parking lot where Seth's truck sat idling.

Seth was behind the wheel, heat blasting through the vents. Cassie sat in the passenger seat, legs tucked under her, a blanket draped over her lap. She looked pale and tense, her eyes glued to the dim hotel lights.

Baxter tapped on the driver's side window.

Seth rolled it down. "What's up?"

Baxter leaned in. "Cassie. You remember the night of the boutique vandalism? You mentioned a black SUV speeding off just as you came downstairs."

Cassie sat up straighter, heart pounding. "Yes. It was the same night they threw bricks through the window."

Baxter nodded. "Kathryn just told us she and Natalie saw a black SUV in her neighborhood multiple times this week. Same build. Same description."

Cassie's eyes widened. "So they were being watched."

"That's what I'm thinking," Baxter said. "Do you remember anything about it? A plate? Even a partial?"

Cassie frowned, then closed her eyes, trying to replay the blur of taillights and panic from that night.

"I'm sorry," she said softly, frustrated. "I only saw the back end. It was already speeding away. All I caught were the taillights."

"No plate?" Baxter asked, not accusing, just hopeful.

She shook her head. "Nothing. I wish I could give you more."

Seth reached over and took her hand. "You gave us plenty. We'll follow the SUV."

Just then, one of the evidence tech deputies emerged from the hotel room carrying a fingerprint case. He approached Baxter quickly.

"Got a few good prints," the deputy said, flipping through the bagged samples. "Most are smudged—hotel staff, probably. But there are a couple clean sets on the inside doorknob and one on the base of the chair."

Baxter raised an eyebrow. "You're going to run them?"

"Already on it. Just uploaded them to the system. If they're in any database, we'll get a ping."

"Let me know the second you do," Baxter said. "This SUV theory's getting legs."

The deputy nodded and headed back to the cruiser.

Baxter turned back to Seth and Cassie. "I'll have a deputy cruise through the Bowen neighborhood again tonight. We'll see if our ghost with tinted windows shows his face again."

Cassie stared back toward the hotel, her voice barely above a whisper.

"I hope we're not already too late."

The soft hum of fluorescent lights filled the quiet squad room. It was well past midnight, and most of the department had gone home for the night, but Baxter sat at his desk, eyes glued to the fingerprint database screen. A mug of stale coffee steamed beside him, untouched.

Then—a ping.

The match came up with a flicker, bold and unmistakable.

NAME: Tate J. Hampton

DOB: 03/17/1990

PRIORS: Theft (x3), Breaking & Entering, Public Intoxication, Disorderly Conduct

Baxter straightened in his chair, squinting at the mugshot.

A wiry man with hollow eyes and a too-proud smirk stared back at him. Tate Hampton.

Not exactly the most dangerous man in the county, but definitely one of the most persistent.

He picked up his radio and called out, "Jackson, you still on site?"

"Affirmative," came the quick reply.

"Get in here. We got a hit."

Moments later, Deputy Jackson pushed through the door. "Print match?"

"Yeah." Baxter turned the monitor toward him. "Tate Hampton. Local dirtbag with a record longer than he is tall."

Jackson leaned in. "I remember him. Loudmouth. Ran his mouth constantly during booking."

Baxter raised an eyebrow. "Go on."

"Couple years back, we brought him in for trespassing. High as a kite. Told me and Patterson that *the bigwigs* paid him to scare people away from Galen Valley. Said they'd always get him out before breakfast."

Baxter leaned back, arms crossed, processing that.

Jackson continued, "At the time, we figured it was drunk talk. Just him puffing up."

"Maybe it wasn't," Baxter said slowly. He clicked into the booking logs. "Let's see who's been bailing him out."

He scrolled through a handful of recent arrests—nothing violent, but enough to paint a pattern.

Every bond posted within hours of arrest. Every time, in cash. Every time, signed by the same name.

BAILED OUT BY: Silas Hampton

Baxter's jaw set.

"Silas Hampton. The father. Owns that rundown supply yard out near Birkinridge house."

"Guy keeps a low profile," Jackson muttered. "But he's got deep roots in the valley."

"Yeah, and now we know he's protecting Tate like a dog guarding its leash."

Baxter stood, grabbed his coat from the back of his chair, and clipped his badge to his belt.

"Time to go pay Daddy-o a visit," he said grimly, already halfway to the door. "See if his boy's curled up at home with him—or hiding a kidnapped journalist in his barn."

Jackson followed. "You want backup?"

"Damn right," Baxter said. "Bring two units. Lights off until I say otherwise. We do this quiet."

As the deputies headed for the cruisers, the night outside swallowed them whole—tense, shadowed, and full of unfinished business.

36

The woods around Birkinridge house near the Hampton place were quieter than usual.

Not the peaceful kind of quiet—but the kind that hummed with warning.

The deputies walked side by side, flashlights in hand, their breath visible in the sharp morning air.

"Anyone else think this feels… too easy?" Jackson muttered.

Baxter said, "I'm counting on that."

Patterson scanned the trees, one hand resting near the weapon on his belt. "If anyone's watching, they already know we're coming. No point being subtle now."

They followed the driveway, one that looked long forgotten by time but preserved just enough to allow trucks to use it—and then all of a sudden, a clearing.

And there it was. The old dilapidated house of Silas Hampton.

A weathered structure, low-roofed and half-covered in ivy, sunken slightly on one side. The porch looked like it would fall in with one step upon it. A rusted generator crouched like a forgotten relic at the corner.

Baxter stopped. "This is Hampton's house? Looks like it is an abandoned shack, where's his truck?"

Jackson stepped up behind Baxter, pointing his flashlight around the yard. It hadn't been mowed and looked like a jungle. He stepped closer to a window at the side of the house and shone his flashlight inside.

All he saw was: darkness, dust, silence.

And then, just beyond the doorway—
Movement.

They found her in the back room.
Natalie.
Tied to a chair, wrists raw but eyes wide open—and burning.
"Are you hurt?"
"Thank God you found me!," Natalie rasped. "I'm fine but they only just left. I think they thought I passed out."
Patterson cut the ropes surrounding her wrists while Baxter and Jackson checked the perimeter. "Who did this to you?"
Natalie looked him straight in the eye.
"Eleanor Hollinger. Not directly but through two men. I don't know their names, they never said them but they kept telling me that Eleanor or Mrs. Hollinger will be really happy with them."
Patterson knelt in front of Natalie so he could cut the ropes around her ankles. "She had you taken?"
"She and her husband," Natalie confirmed. "I got too close. Found records of a second land transfer—one that tied Pinewood Capital directly to laundering federal education grants. I was trying to get all the information to give to Cassie Dixon when they grabbed me."
Patterson helped her to her feet. "We've got you. You're safe now."
"Thank you," Natalie said, her voice shaking.
"There's no one out there," said Baxter as he and Jackson came back inside. "Let's get her out of here and to the hospital then we will cordon this place off and start looking for the Hamptons."
"You will find them at the Hollinger's," said Natalie, "they caretake their estate and live in the servant's quarters."
"She told me the Hollingers paid them to kidnap her and bring her here," Patterson chimed in on the conversation.

"Well, I will need a search warrant to go there," replied Baxter, "if we don't do it by the book with the Hollingers, they will weasel their way out."

"Why can't we just go and arrest the Hamptons for kidnapping Natalie?" asked Jackson, "after all we just found her tied up here in their house."

"Nope," said Baxter, "with the Hollingers being involved, I want a judge to sign off on a search warrant."

The dashboard clock glowed softly as Seth and Cassie sat in the warmth of the idling truck, the chill of the evening pressing against the windows. Cassie, bundled in a blanket, stared out into the dark parking lot, her thoughts heavy.

Seth's phone buzzed, breaking the silence. He glanced at the screen.

"Ross, what's the news?"

Cassie turned to him, eyes wide with anticipation.

"That's incredible. Thank you for the update."

He ended the call and turned to Cassie.

"They found her. Natalie's alive and en route to the hospital. Baxter said she is shaken up but seems to be ok."

Cassie's eyes welled up with tears of relief.

"Thank God," she said, "Let's go."

As Seth pulled out of the parking lot, Cassie quickly dialed Kathryn.

"Kathryn, they found Natalie," she told her. "She's safe and heading to the hospital now."

Kathryn's voice, though faint over the phone, carried immense relief.

"That's the best news I've heard all day. Thank you for letting me know."

Cassie then called Elliot, sharing the good news.

"Elliot, Natalie's been found," she told him. "She's on her way to the hospital."

"That's a relief," he said, "I'll head there now."

Cassie ended the call, leaning back in her seat, a smile breaking through her earlier worry.

"I can't wait to see her," Cassie said, reaching over and grabbing Seth's hand.

'Neither can I," he replied, as he gave her hand a gentle squeeze.

The sterile scent of antiseptics filled the air as fluorescent lights cast a soft glow over the bustling emergency room. Nurses moved swiftly between curtained bays, their footsteps muffled by the linoleum floor.

Cassie sat beside Natalie's hospital bed, her eyes scanning the monitors that beeped steadily, offering a rhythmic assurance of life. Natalie, though pale and bruised, managed a weak smile as she reached out to grasp Cassie's hand.

"You came."

"Of course I did," said Cassie, "we were all so worried."

A nurse entered, checking the IV line and jotting notes on a clipboard.

"The doctor has ordered an MRI to rule out any internal injuries from the head trauma," she told Natalie, "we'll take you down shortly."

"Thank you."

As the nurse exited, leaving them alone, Natalie turned to Cassie, her voice barely above a whisper.

"Cassie, while I was... held, I kept thinking about everything we've uncovered. There's more—about Marshall Bowen."

"What do you mean?" asked Cassie.

"He wasn't just complicit; he was orchestrating it. After taking over the sheriff's department, he ensured the founding families' criminal activities remained hidden. He appointed deputies who would look the other way, sabotaged investigations, laundered money, and enforced land grabs."

Cassie's eyes widened, the weight of Natalie's words sinking in.

"This goes much deeper than we thought."

"Yes it does," Natalie said, 'and it traces back to one of the first sheriffs in Galen Valley. Guess which family's name keeps appearing?"

"Carrow?"

Natalie's eyebrows shot up in surprise.

"You knew?"

"I just found out."

Before Natalie could respond, an orderly entered with a wheelchair.

"Ms. Oliver," he said, "we're ready for your MRI."

Cassie stood, gently squeezing Natalie's hand.

"We'll talk more after your scan."

"Be careful, Cassie. They're watching everyone."

Cassie nodded, her mind racing with the implications of Natalie's revelations as she watched her friend being wheeled away.

37

The arrest warrant for Mayor Denise Carrow was issued by noon.

Seth watched from across the street as federal agents escorted her from Town Hall. No cuffs. No resistance.

Meanwhile, Baxter stood at the edge of the Hollinger's circular driveway, his arms crossed over his chest. The air was thick with anticipation as unmarked federal vehicles lined the perimeter.

A team of federal agents, clad in tactical gear, approached the ornate front door. With practiced precision, they knocked sharply. Moments later, the door opened to reveal a surprised Hollinger patriarch, his silk robe hastily tied.

"Henry Hollinger, you're under arrest for conspiracy, obstruction of justice, and racketeering."

Before the elder Hollinger could protest, agents stepped forward, securing his wrists in cuffs.

Inside the estate, agents moved swiftly, detaining Eleanor Hollinger. They also entered the servant quarters and arrested Silas Hampton and his son, Tate, for aiding and abetting criminal activities, including kidnapping and intimidation."

Baxter watched as the once-powerful figures of Galen Valley were led out of their estate with their heads bowed. The weight of justice pressed heavily upon them.

As the federal vehicles departed, Baxter took a deep breath, the cool morning air filling his lungs. The long-standing shadow over Galen Valley was beginning to lift.

The message was clear.

No one was untouchable anymore.

Cassie sat in the Everbrew café with Kathryn sipping her coffee without flinching, her laptop open, cursor blinking at the top of a new article.

Not about pain.

Not about the past.

About rebuilding.

Across the table, Natalie was typing just as furiously.

"So," Natalie said, "how does it feel to not be the town scandal anymore?"

Cassie laughed. "Don't kid yourself, we're all the scandal now."

"Look who's here," Kathryn exclaimed as Elliot joined them at the table.

"I booked my flight," he said.

Cassie nodded. "L.A."

"Yeah."

"I'm proud of you," Kathryn told him. "Pursuing your dreams."

He smiled. "I'm excited for the future, I have been in contact with friends who said they can help me get my foot in the door out there."

"It will take a lot of patience," Natalie said softly. "But if anyone can be successful out there, Elliot, I believe it's you."

Elliot nodded, eyes shining.

"Thank you ladies, I don't think you realize how much all of you mean to me. I will miss you all very much"

"No you won't," said Kathryn, "you will get out there with those glam starlets and forget all about us small town girlies."

"Not a chance," Elliot replied as he hugged each of them before turning and walking out the door.

Across the country, in a San Diego hotel, Devon Blake watched the coverage unfold.

Cassie's interview. Denise's arrest. The unraveling of the Hollinger name after Natalie's kidnapping.

He poured a drink and stared at the news with a sneer.

They were supposed to break.

He picked up his phone, dialed a private number.

A pause.

"Are the assets still viable?" he asked.

Another pause.

"Then we regroup."

He hung up.

And smiled.

Because even if Cassie and Natalie had won the battle…

Devon wasn't done with Galen Valley.

Not yet.

The next day, Cassie found two plain white envelopes in her mailbox among the utility bills, credit card offers and local sales flyers.

No return address on either one.

Inside the first one: a letter. Handwritten. The penmanship elegant. The name at the bottom chilled her.

Clara Hollinger. Henry and Eleanor's daughter.

Cassie sat down on the front porch steps and read:

"I don't expect forgiveness. I only ask that you know—some of us were raised in the shadow of this town's sins. We were taught to protect things we didn't understand. And now that the curtain has been ripped down, maybe there's still time to build something better."

Attached was a copy of a notarized affidavit—one that listed several *off-record* meetings between Denise Carrow, the Hollinger family, and Devon Blake.

Cassie could not believe what she was holding. This isn't just an ending. It's an opportunity she thought to herself.

To start over. *The right way.*

She opened the second envelope to find just a photo.

Devon Blake.

Standing in front of a building with a Pinewood Capital banner behind him.

And written in pen at the bottom:

"Round two."

Later that evening as Seth and Cassie enjoyed dinner together he said, "I heard Elliot left."

Cassie nodded. "Yes, he is headed to L.A."

Seth nodded. "To start over?"

She smiled. "Actually, yeah. I think that's exactly what he plans to do."

He studied her. "And do... what?"

Cassie looked up and met Seth's eyes. "To direct, act, sell the script he wrote."

Then, without hesitation, she reached for his hand.

"Let's not talk about him anymore, let's talk about us. I am sorry for all we have been through but I can't say I regret it. We have grown because of it, become closer and understand each other better now. I no longer feel like the caged woman wanting to escape Galen Valley or the troubled woman they were trying to chase out of town. I feel like and want to be the woman who *builds it back.* With you beside me."

Seth didn't say anything.

He just leaned in—and kissed her.

Soft.

Certain.

A promise.

The next day, Cassie walked into Town Hall—not as a witness, not as a warning, but as a candidate.

Kathryn and Natalie stood behind her. Seth stood beside her.

Reporters turned. Cameras clicked.

And Cassie smiled.

"I'm here to file my candidacy for Mayor of Galen Valley."

Gasps. Cheers. And from the back of the room—Celia Beaumont, quietly nodding and smiling.

The town wasn't healed.

It was scarred. Raw. Still rumbling with aftershocks.

But this time, Cassie wasn't running.

She was walking forward.

With all the ghosts behind her.

And a future waiting to be written.

38

Cassie didn't sleep the night before the town forum.

She paced. She wrote. She rewrote.

And when dawn broke over Galen Valley, her speech wasn't polished—but it was *true*.

By early evening, the community center was packed—standing room only. Reporters lined the back wall, residents filled the pews, and curious tourists filtered in, lured by the town's now-national drama.

Across the stage stood two other candidates: a former school principal backed by the old business association, and a councilwoman who had stayed painfully silent through all of Galen Valley's chaos.

Cassie sat between them, calm but electric.

Natalie was in the front row. Kathryn and Celia sat beside her. Seth lingered by the door, arms crossed, protective, proud.

Moderator Jim Fowler, a retired judge and longtime town resident, cleared his throat at the mic.

"Each candidate will have five minutes to speak. Mrs. Dixon, you may begin."

Cassie stood, walked to the podium, and looked out at the town that she had wanted to run from and then had tried to chew her up and spit her out.

She didn't use notes.

She didn't need to.

"I didn't grow up here," she began. "I wasn't born into one of the founding families. And for a long time, I did not feel like I belonged in Galen Valley. I spent a lot of time planning my escape but then all that changed when people tried to run me out of town. I realized that I do belong and have every right to be here just as much as the next person. Maybe that's exactly why I'm standing here today."

A murmur rippled through the room.

"I've seen this town at its worst. I've seen what happens when good people say nothing and power hides behind legacy. And I know what it feels like to be afraid—to lose everything because the truth was too loud for comfort."

Cassie paused, letting that settle.

"But I also know what this place can be."

She looked toward Celia.

"A town where accountability matters more than bloodlines. Where history is honored but not weaponized. Where secrets don't decide our future."

A few people clapped. Someone in the back stood.

Cassie didn't rush. She let her voice grow stronger.

"I'm not running for mayor because I have all the answers. I'm running because I'm finally asking the *right questions*. The ones this town has buried for far too long."

She looked around the room, her eyes settling on the undecideds, the skeptics.

"I know I'm not what some of you expected. But maybe Galen Valley doesn't need another politician. Maybe it needs a survivor. A builder. A *fighter*."

More applause. Louder now.

"I've already stood in the fire for this town. And I'm still here. Not because I have to be... but because I *choose* to be."

She stepped back from the mic.

Silence.

Then—

Thunderous applause.

Later that night, Cassie sat on the front porch of her house with Seth beside her.

"You really shook them," he said.

She leaned against his shoulder. "You think it was enough?"

"I think," he said, "you just changed the whole election."

A pause.

"And maybe the town."

Cassie looked up at the stars overhead.

"I don't want to win because I survived something awful," she said. "I want to win because I *believe* in something better."

Seth kissed her temple. "Then you already have."

But elsewhere in Galen Valley, a phone call crackled through an encrypted line.

"She's gaining momentum," the voice said.

A man answered on the other end.

"She'll never make it to Election Day."

A click.

And silence.

The posters went up overnight.

They were slapped on telephone poles, community boards, and the windows of shuttered businesses including Valley Vogue.

Cassie saw them on her way to the coffee shop to meet Natalie and Kathryn—black-and-white, grainy photos of her standing beside Devon Blake from nearly a decade ago. The headline scrawled in bold red across the top:

"She's Not Who You Think She Is."

Below it: half-truths. Twisted timelines. Edited excerpts from old news coverage. No official source. No group claiming responsibility.

Just poison.

Made to look like truth.

"Cowards," Natalie spat, tossing one of the posters on the table they circled around inside Everbrew cafe. "This isn't a campaign—it's a hit job."

Cassie stood beside her, jaw tight, heart pounding. "They want people to forget everything we've exposed. They want them scared again."

Kathryn pulled out her phone. "I already called the city cleanup crew. But this isn't just street propaganda. Someone's spending *real* money to get these printed and distributed."

Cassie looked toward the window, where two more posters had already been torn down by a local shop owner.

"We need to find out *who*."

Seth was already working on it and had reached out to the one man he knew could find out.

Baxter Ross's appointment as acting sheriff had come swiftly after Denise Carrow's arrest, and he told Seth he planned to use it like a scalpel. Quiet. Precise.

That morning, Baxter had pulled surveillance footage from a street cam near one of the larger poster drops.

There, just after midnight—two familiar figures moved in the shadows.

Hooded. Gloved.

But unmistakably, Langston and Daines

The same men who had slow walked the Griggs disappearance case and suppressed evidence.

Baxter leaned back in his chair and called Seth.

"Looks like the same crew is still playing cleanup," Baxter muttered as Seth answered. "Even now."

Seth leaned against the hood of his truck, parked behind the ranger station, the cold steel beneath him grounding him against the surge of anger boiling in his chest. "What crew?"

Baxter's voice on the other end was laced with disgust. "Langston and Daines. They're the culprits putting up those posters all over town targeting Cassie's campaign. Sure they are filled with lies, personal attacks, twisted quotes—hell, even a fake endorsement from a felon. It's amateur-hour smear tactics, but effective in a town already on edge."

Seth swore under his breath. "They're still trying to tear her down—after everything."

"They're doing more than that," Baxter said. "I pulled their files. Started cross-referencing activity logs, call records, expense reports. Let's just say… the posters are the *least* of their crimes."

Seth straightened. "You think it goes beyond dirty politics?"

"I know it does," Baxter said grimly. "There's a pattern of abuse of power, falsified reports, obstruction—hell, they buried half of Marshall's internal investigations before he even took his own fall. I've already called in the Bureau."

Seth raised an eyebrow. "You brought in the FBI?"

"I'm the acting sheriff now," Baxter replied. "It's my mess to clean up, and I'm not about to let it keep spreading."

Seth paced along the gravel, the cold wind biting through his coat. "You think they'll act on it?"

"They already have," Baxter said. "I gave them full access to Langston and Daines' case files this morning. Less than three hours later, they sent over an arrest team. Said the pattern was clear: coordinated corruption, abuse of authority, and potential federal violations tied to racketeering and civil rights obstruction."

Seth let out a low whistle. "That fast, huh?"

"They barely had to scratch the surface."

There was a pause.

Then Baxter added, "I'm riding with the agents to Langston's place now. He won't see it coming."

Seth nodded, his jaw tight. "If you're ok with it, I'll go with the other team to Daines' house. It's time he answers for everything."

"Just keep it clean," Baxter said. "I want them in cuffs—not giving anyone else more trouble."

"They won't get any sympathy from me," Seth replied. "But they will get justice."

The line went silent for a moment—just the sound of the wind and the hum of both men realizing that the tide had truly turned.

Finally, Baxter said, "Alright, see you at the sheriff department."

"Yeah," Seth said. "With both of them in custody."

As the call ended, Seth climbed into his truck and pulled onto the road—driving straight into the future with purpose.

39

A short while later, Baxter stood in Langston's front yard with two FBI agents and an arrest warrant. Not far away, Seth and two other FBI agents were at the home of Daines with an arrest warrant in his name.

Neither one resisted.

But as Daines was cuffed, he looked straight at Seth and smiled.

"You think this ends with her in charge? You think the town's ready for that?"

Seth didn't answer.

Because he didn't *care* if the town was ready.

Cassie was.

And that was enough.

Kathryn, Natalie and Cassie entered the boutique the next morning to find someone had slid a postcard under the door.

On the front: a photograph of the old trailhead where Tyler Griggs had died.

On the back, handwritten in sharp black ink:

"You may have cleared your name. But you'll never clean this town."

Cassie stared at it for a long time.

Then tossed it in the trash.

Because fear was a language she no longer spoke.

The boutique still bore the scars of chaos—broken display racks in the corner, boards across the front windows, and a lingering smell of scorched wood.

But today, the *ladies were back*—not just to reminisce or clean up, but to decide what came next.

Cassie set a fresh coffee on the front counter and passed another to Natalie, who leaned against one of the clothing racks draped with plastic sheeting. Kathryn stood at the center of the space, arms crossed, gaze sweeping the room she'd once poured her soul into.

"So," Kathryn said, exhaling slowly, "do I fix it up and reopen... or close the doors for good?"

Cassie and Natalie exchanged a glance.

"You don't have to decide today," Cassie said gently. "But you should know—this place *still matters.*"

"Not just to you," Natalie added. "To this whole town."

Kathryn let out a dry laugh, folding her arms. "Does this town *deserve* it?"

Cassie gave her a sympathetic smile. "Some of it does."

They all stood in silence for a beat, sipping coffee, taking in the quiet. Outside, the town was starting to stir—though today it felt different. Lighter. As if the very air in Galen Valley had shifted.

"I still can't believe it," Natalie said, breaking the quiet. "Langston and Daines. Arrested. Marched off their porches by federal agents like characters in a bad political drama."

"Yeah," Kathryn said, her voice low. "And to think... they were once the ones we trusted to uphold justice."

Cassie frowned. "I guess I always thought corruption was something that happened in the big cities like Chicago and not small towns like this one."

Natalie took a slow sip of her coffee. "Power doesn't care how big the town is. If there's influence to be bought or secrets to be protected, people will find a way. Dirty politics isn't just for Washington."

Kathryn walked slowly to the cracked mirror that had once reflected smiling customers in dresses and designer scarves. Now, a thin fracture ran through the center like a wound in glass.

"I built this boutique to be a haven," she said. "For women to feel beautiful. For me to feel *independent*. And it became something else... part of a target."

"But it wasn't the boutique's fault," Cassie said gently. "It was theirs. Their fear of strong women. Their fear of change."

Kathryn looked at her. "You mean *your* mayoral campaign?"

Cassie nodded. "I think we rattled the whole structure."

Natalie smiled faintly. "And then knocked it over."

They all laughed softly—tired, but unified.

Kathryn turned back toward the dressing rooms, the hanging velvet curtain still slightly singed at the bottom corner. "Maybe it needs a fresh coat of paint. New windows. Some bolder inventory. A full rebrand."

Cassie lit up. "Valley Vogue 2.0?"

Kathryn smirked. "Maybe. But with sprinklers and an alarm system that could wake the *dead*."

Natalie raised her coffee in a mock toast. "To rebuilding what matters."

Cassie raised hers. "To starting over stronger."

Kathryn clinked her cup against theirs. "To *not letting the bastards win*."

And in that quiet, wounded space, surrounded by broken glass, peeled paint, and possibility—they made the unspoken decision to move forward.

Together.

A few weeks later, Cassie stood in front of the boutique's mirror, adjusting the navy blazer she planned to wear to the final debate. It had been Kathryn's idea—"Mayoral but not matronly," she'd said. Commanding, without trying too hard.

Cassie barely recognized herself anymore.

Not because of how she looked—but because of how she *felt*.

Clear. Calm. Certain.

She wasn't defending herself now.

She was *defining* herself.

Across town, Seth stood in the backroom of the sheriff's office, reviewing surveillance records, financial logs, and one final report that had been buried beneath Devon Blake's web of shell companies.

He finally found it.

A land acquisition proposal.

Not for Wren Hollow.

Not for the town square.

But for Galen Valley Regional Medical Center.

Devon hadn't just wanted to own the land.

He wanted the *infrastructure*—the hospital, the school, the water systems.

Everything beneath the town's feet.

And in the final paragraph: a recommendation.

"Local control not essential. Influence through campaign support and strategic board placement recommended."

Devon hadn't been planning to destroy Galen Valley.

He was planning to *own* it.

At the debate, Cassie stepped on stage to thunderous applause.

She was composed, with her hands folded at the podium, eyes focused. Her opponents flanked her: the councilwoman, rattled and stiff; and the school principal, now openly backed by surviving Hollinger allies.

They weren't interested in unity.

They wanted preservation.

Cassie wanted progress.

The first few questions were expected—taxes, education, infrastructure.

But then came the pivot.

"Mrs. Dixon," the moderator asked, "how do you respond to accusations that your campaign is fueled by vengeance?"

Cassie leaned forward.

"I'm not running to get even," she said. "I'm running to get *better*. Better schools. Better leadership. Better truth. And a town where no one else has to survive what I did just to be heard."

Applause erupted. Her opponents shifted uncomfortably.

"You can cling to tradition," she added, "or you can build a future. But you *can't do both.*"

An hour later, the debate ended.

Cassie stepped off stage to cheers, handshakes, and questions. She spotted Seth near the edge of the crowd, nodding, holding up a folder.

"We need to talk," he said. "Now."

In Valley Vogue's back office, Cassie flipped through the latest documents.

"The hospital?" she asked, stunned.

Seth nodded. "Devon had people lined up to privatize key infrastructure in town. The same people who donated anonymously to your opponents."

Cassie stared at the pages, something cold forming in her gut.

"It was never just about reputation. He wanted to *replace* Galen Valley. Piece by piece."

Seth put a hand on her shoulder. "You stopped him."

She looked up at him.

"Not yet."

Then came the explosion.
It happened just after midnight.

40

The *Everbrew Café*—the heart of the town's downtown stretch—was reduced to smoke and flame in a single, deafening blast.

The sound echoed across Galen Valley, waking every resident.

Cassie and Seth reached the scene within minutes.

Firefighters were already battling the blaze.

Natalie stood nearby, stunned, ash smudged across her cheek. She had moved into the apartment above the boutique and was sitting on her balcony when the explosion happened.

"It was intentional," she said. "I saw a figure run just before it happened. They knew."

Seth stepped aside to take a call—and returned, his face pale.

"It was a message," he said quietly.

He handed Cassie his phone.

A text. Untraceable.

"Last warning. Drop out, or more burns."

Cassie didn't look away from the screen.

"I'm not dropping anything," she said. "Not the truth. Not the town. *Not now.*"

Cassie's voice rang with fierce clarity, the conviction in her words hanging in the cool air like a battle cry. Seth stood beside her, his hand resting lightly on her back, steady and silent. Around them, the damage lingered—the cracked glass, the scorched signage, the debris.

From behind them, the measured sound of boots crunching gravel drew their attention.

Baxter approached, his sheriff's jacket unzipped, the weight of responsibility clear in the lines around his eyes. He'd heard her—every word.

"Of course you're not dropping out," Baxter said firmly as he joined them. "Hell, Cassie, you shouldn't. This—" he gestured toward the destroyed cafe, the shattered storefront, the town itself, "—this is exactly why you have to stay in the race."

Cassie met his gaze, searching for doubt and finding none.

Baxter continued, voice low and urgent. "And you standing your ground gives me something I can work with. Declaring a state of emergency. Now I've got justification. I'm calling the governor."

Seth straightened. "For what?"

"To bring in the National Guard," Baxter said. "For public safety. For order. Until this election is over. And until the people responsible for *this*," he motioned to the town square now wrapped in yellow tape, "are behind bars. Not just the ones tossing bricks and explosives or putting up slander posters. The *top brass*. The ones issuing orders in back rooms, not getting their hands dirty."

Cassie's eyes widened. "You think the attacks were ordered by someone higher up?"

Baxter nodded. "Absolutely. This has the stink of orchestration. These aren't just impulsive threats anymore. They're escalations."

Seth's jaw tightened. "Do we have any idea who's pulling the strings?"

Baxter glanced toward the nearby traffic light camera perched above the square, its red light blinking faintly.

"Cameras," he said. "Downtown. Side streets. That new one the library installed last year. If they're dumb enough to keep operating in a town full of cameras, we'll find them."

Cassie folded her arms, still shaking slightly from all of it but grounded by resolve. "And if they're not on the cameras?"

"Then we dig deeper," Baxter replied. "Follow the money. Track who paid for the flyers. Who gave Langston and Daines their orders. And we *will* find the paper trail."

He stepped closer, lowering his voice just enough so that only the two of them could hear.

"But I need you to keep being the lighthouse. You're what's giving people hope right now. If you step down, they win. If you stay... the town might just find its way back."

Cassie looked between them—Baxter, the once-gruff lawman who now carried a battered kind of hope, and Seth, the man who'd walked through fire for her, still standing beside her like a shield.

She gave a single, slow nod.

"I am definitely staying in the fight," she said.

Baxter smiled faintly, then turned, already pulling out his phone as he walked away, dialing the governor's office before he even reached his cruiser.

Cassie watched him go, the full weight of the moment settling on her shoulders—but this time, she didn't feel it alone.

Seth stepped closer and whispered, "You've got this."

Cassie nodded, her gaze turning back toward the broken streets of Galen Valley, voice steady as steel.

"Let's finish what they started."

Cassie turned from the stove and headed to the kitchen table with the casserole dish she had just removed from the oven when her phone buzzed on the counter.

She set it down and went to check her phone. It was a text from Baxter.

Got him. Devon's in custody. So are four of his goons. I'll explain more in the morning, but he's headed to federal holding. We got him, Cass. We got all of them.

Cassie sank slowly into a chair, a wave of relief washing over her so intense it left her momentarily speechless.

A beat later, she called out, "Seth!"

He stepped into the room, towel over his shoulder, fresh from the shower, looking concerned until he saw the expression on her face.

"What is it?"

Cassie looked up, her eyes bright with both disbelief and satisfaction. "They got Devon. And the men he brought from Chicago. Baxter arrested all of them—today. Just handed them over to federal custody. He said they're being charged not just for what they did here, but for similar operations in other small towns."

Seth exhaled, visibly stunned, then crossed the room in three strides and wrapped her in a tight hug.

"They're really gone," he said into her hair. "Finally."

"They can't touch this town now," she whispered.

They held onto each other for a long, quiet moment, and when they finally pulled apart, Cassie smiled. "Want to go sit on the porch for a bit after dinner?"

Seth nodded. "Absolutely."

The porch lights were dim, casting a soft golden glow over the two rocking chairs where Cassie and Seth now sat, hands loosely intertwined as crickets chirped around them.

A bottle of red wine sat between them, mostly untouched. Two glasses, full.

Cassie took a deep breath, letting the scent of the night air and the distant hum of the town settle in her bones.

"Do you think tomorrow changes everything?" she asked softly.

Seth tilted his head. "I think tomorrow *proves* that things have already changed."

She glanced over at him. "You think I'm ready?"

"I think," he said, "you've been ready for a long time. You just finally believe it."

They sat in silence for a while, the stars coming out slowly above Galen Valley.

"Tomorrow," Cassie said, lifting her glass, "we vote."

"And win," Seth added, clinking his glass gently against hers.

They sipped in unison, letting the quiet wrap around them like a warm blanket.

No speeches. No crowds. Just the two of them—on the eve of a new chapter neither of them could have imagined when they first stepped foot into this town as husband and wife.

Cassie looked out toward the horizon, a single thought rising in her mind:

Whatever comes next, I'm ready.

41

The town was quiet on Election Day.

Not peaceful.

Braced.

Cassie stood on the steps of Valley Vogue just after sunrise, coffee in one hand, voter list in the other. She had walked these streets when people crossed them to avoid her. Now, passersby nodded, smiled, even honked as they drove past.

She didn't let it swell her pride.

She let it anchor her resolve.

At the polling station, lines stretched down the block—more people than anyone expected. First-timers. Elderly voters in wheelchairs. Teenagers with "I Voted" stickers plastered on jackets.

Cassie stood beside Seth, watching the turnout.

"This isn't just about politics," he said quietly.

"No," she agreed. "It's about *trust.*"

He smiled. "And they're trusting you."

She turned toward him, eyes full of memory, fire, and something else.

"We made it, didn't we?"

"We're making it," he said.

And then he kissed her—quick, certain, and *public.*

Because they had nothing left to hide.

Cassie waited in the boutique with Kathryn, Celia, and a handful of supporters as the sun set and the vote count began.

She didn't pace.

She didn't bite her nails.

She simply *waited*.

Then the results came in.

And Galen Valley made its choice.

She won.

Not by a landslide.

But by enough.

Enough to shift the course of everything.

Cheers erupted in the square. Reporters called. Strangers cried. Kathryn opened champagne again, and Natalie yelled something about writing a book.

But Cassie?

She stepped outside the back of the boutique and looked up at the stars.

She didn't feel triumphant.

She felt *ready*.

Seth joined her, his smile tired but genuine.

"Madam Mayor," he said, mock-formal.

"Don't you start," she teased.

He wrapped an arm around her. "You did it."

"No," she said. "*We* did."

The following morning, Cassie gave her first speech as mayor-elect from the steps of Sage Hill, where Galen Beaumont once imagined a town that could outlive his name.

"I know where we've been," she said. "I know what we've buried. But I also know this—truth is not the enemy of tradition. It's the *foundation* of real legacy."

She paused, scanning the faces of a town that had hated her, hunted her, and now... believed her.

"From this day forward, Galen Valley won't be a town built on silence. It will be a town built on *voices.* All of them."

Later that night, Cassie opened a letter that had been delivered to Valley Vogue but addressed to her.

It was short.

"You always were the strongest one. Be the light, Cass. The town doesn't need saving—it needs someone who believes it can be better. That someone is you."

Elliot

She smiled, folded the letter, and placed it in her desk.

Then she joined Seth on the front porch.

She felt uncaged, content and at home.

Epilogue

Six months later...
The streets of Galen Valley looked different now.

New street lamps lined the square. The Hollinger name had been removed from the public library. A community arts fund had been established in Tyler Griggs' memory. And the newly rebuilt Everbrew Café was packed every weekend with students, families, and the curious newcomers drawn in by the headlines and hope.

At the center of it all was Mayor Cassie Dixon.

She walked with a clipboard tucked under one arm, greeting townspeople by name, smiling as kids on bikes waved from the sidewalk.

The scars weren't gone.

But they were healing.

That afternoon, the sun slanted across the antique desk in the newly refurbished mayor's office, its golden rays catching on the crystal nameplate that read: Mayor Cassandra Dixon. The room still held the scent of fresh paint and ambition. Cassie had barely settled in—still getting used to the hum of government, the constant emails, and the low murmur of voices outside her office door.

She was reviewing a draft of a community grant proposal when Darlene, her assistant, appeared in the doorway holding an envelope.

"This just came for you," Darlene said, her brow furrowed. "No stamp. Someone must've hand-delivered it."

Cassie took it with a small frown. The envelope was unmarked except for her name, printed in blocky, unfamiliar letters. No return address. No seal. Just thick, off-white paper—like something pulled from a typewriter era.

She waited until the door closed behind Darlene, then carefully slid a finger under the flap.

Inside: a single sheet of paper, folded once.

No signature. No heading.

Only a chilling message typed in black ink:

Mayor Dixon,
Congratulations on your new office.
But beware—there is someone within your administration who is not who they appear to be.
Everyone has skeletons in the closet.
Some are just buried deeper than others.
Be prepared, Mayor Dixon. Your office will be in turmoil.
It's coming soon.

Cassie stared at the page, her fingers tightening around its edges.

No clue who sent it. No specific accusation. Just a threat veiled in formality.

Her heartbeat quickened—not from fear, but from something sharper.

Someone inside? she thought. *But who?*

Her mind raced through faces. Appointees. Staffers. Allies from the campaign. People she *trusted.*

The room suddenly felt colder.

She folded the letter and slid it back into the envelope, locking it in the top drawer of her desk. Then she stood and crossed to the window, staring out over the town square—where signs of rebuilding still stood beside fresh new hope.

Cassie's jaw set.

They'd tried to destroy her once. They'd failed.

But this time, the enemy wouldn't be outside the gates.

They'd be inside.

And she'd be ready.

Thank You for Reading

Dear Reader,

Thank you so much for joining me on this journey through *Galen Valley Chronicles*. This series was born from a desire to explore the lives of the people who once lived on the edges of the *Secrets of Sage Manor* storyline—those supporting characters who, as it turns out, had powerful stories and secrets of their own waiting to be told.

As the world of Sage Manor grew, I realized that Galen Valley wasn't just a setting—it was a community full of layered, complex individuals navigating love, loss, ambition, and redemption. It became clear they deserved their own spotlight.

Readers of *Secrets of Sage Manor* will find familiar faces peppered throughout these pages, because just as the residents of Galen Valley support the Beaumonts, the Beaumont family supports Galen Valley. It takes *everyone* to create a community.

I hope you've enjoyed unraveling the lives and secrets of the people who call Galen Valley home. It may be a small town—but its stories are many, and its secrets even more plentiful.

Stay tuned… there's so much more to come.

With heartfelt thanks,

LG Rice
Author of *Secrets of Sage Manor & Galen Valley Chronicles*

For updates on new book releases, exclusive discounts, and behind-the-scenes content, please visit www.authorlgrice.com and subscribe to the newsletter.

Contact me at: hello@authorlgrice.com

www.ingramcontent.com/pod-product-compliance
Lightning Source LLC
Chambersburg PA
CBHW070601120726
47909CB00007B/2406